AN AFRICAN ORCHARD

Mavis Pachter

TSL Publications

First published in Great Britain in 2021
By TSL Publications, Rickmansworth

Copyright © 2021 Mavis Pachter

ISBN / 978-1-914245-20-6

Cover image by Lise Taylor-Vebel

DEDICATION

I dedicate this book to those who flee from war and injustice
And seek a country where they may live in peace.

1886

"Love flickered and glowed in the dying embers of a schtetl (village) once called home".

Miriam sat beside Joseph beneath an apple tree in full bloom with its sweet scent pervading the air. The fields around her were covered in flowers and cattle grazed contentedly nearby. Although it was the beginning of spring she felt a chill in the air.

"Joseph, what's a pogrom?" she asked in a hushed voice leaning in towards him. I overheard two people talking in the village."

"Ask your Papa," he said standing up and glancing at rain clouds hovering above them. "We'd better go home it looks like it could rain any minute."

"Why won't you tell me?" She reached out to touch his hand. "We always tell each other everything."

Joseph shook his head as he helped her up and then pulled her towards him and kissed her. He took something out of his pocket closing her hand over the item. "I made this for you." His voice was hoarse as he ran his hand over her silken hair. He breathed in deeply and cupped her face in his hands. "Miriam, you'll always have a special place in my heart."

Miriam, taken by surprise, lost her balance and Joseph steadied her as she looked at a small heart carved out of wood. She could hardly breathe as she whispered, "It's beautiful, Joseph." She was aware of him in a way she had never been before. Her eyes sought his as she admired his newly grown beard and how grown up it made him look. Together they walked home hand in hand, and Miriam found herself unable to stop talking. "Papa says we'll all be together on Friday night. I'm going to wear a new dress that Papa bought me for special occasions." She glanced at him puzzled as he disengaged his hand from hers when they reached their village. They walked past wooden houses standing side by side with smoke curling out of chimneys. Passing the bakers where an aroma of freshly baked bread wafted towards them, next to which was the butcher both of which were ramshackle huts. The synagogue was a larger wooden house and all stood on the same street which was beginning to turn muddy from the rain. They turned a corner to a street where they both lived in wooden houses built in higgledy piggledy fashion. Miriam glanced at Joseph again who remained silent. She stood watching him as he waved goodbye and blew her a kiss before going into his house. She ran towards her house with her heart hammering in her chest not bothering about her skirt dragging on wet muddy ground.

The last of the embers were flickering in the fireplace. Miriam's mother, Becky, stood at a rickety old table making gooseberry preserve.

"Where have you been Miriam? Look at the mud on your skirt," and tut tutted. "We need more wood. Go fetch some Miriam."

"I told you I was meeting Joseph Mama. Do I have to go out? It's raining." Getting no answer she was just about to go back out when her father, Avraham, walked in.

"I'll go Miriam. You'll get soaked," said Avraham.

"Thank you, Papa." Miriam set to brewing their tea and could only think of Joseph's kiss.

Avraham returned and lit the logs on the fire. Rubbing his back he slumped in his chair by the fireside. "Must be a way to earn a better living. One day we'll have a bigger house so you don't have to sleep in our living room, Miriam."

"Papa, our home is cosy. I like sleeping near the hearth and I love the smell of a wood fire." Miriam bent over and kissed his cheek.

"Isn't that tea ready yet Miriam?" her mother asked. "What's the matter with you tonight?"

Miriam was lost in thought, and didn't pay much attention to her mother who was always chiding her about something or other. Her father was much easier to please. His booming voice cut through her thoughts and she placed the teapot on the table almost spilling the contents thinking about Joseph.

Avraham looked at the meagre dish of meat that Becky had cooked. "I wish I could provide more meat for the Sabbath table, then you wouldn't have to slice it paper thin," he said, almost knocking over the teapot.

Becky raised her voice. "Be careful. You're always knocking things over with those clumsy hands of yours. Wasn't it your mother who said such hands could have been those of a doctor? God bless her, she's probably looking down on me now from heaven and shaking a finger. Miriam, don't just stand there. Why are you staring out of the window? Be useful, go next door and ask Rachel for a little sour milk."

Miriam was happy to have any excuse to go to Joseph's house. She brushed her hair, put on a clean skirt and hurried out before her mother started complaining again.

Becky waited for Miriam to go. "Must you talk in front of Miriam? She's only a child."

"Nonsense, she's sixteen and no one remains a child for long living here. You can't hide what's happening to us. May Alexander be persecuted as he's persecuted us," and spat. "Life in the Schtetl is no different to when our parents lived here. I'm going to evening prayers, Becky."

"Well, don't forget to ask God for a little more meat for the Sabbath," and raised her eyes to heaven.

Miriam was met by Rachel, Joseph's mother, as she walked up the path to their house.

"Mama sent me to ask for a little sour milk."

"Of course, but come inside and say hello to Sarah," said Rachel closing the front door. She poured sour milk into a small bowl and called out, "Sarah, Miriam's here."

Sarah shuffled in patting her grey hair into place and exclaimed, "My favourite young girl. But you look lovely, Miriam. You've done something to your hair? Ah, a plait. I like it and such a pretty blue skirt and that tiny waist. I once had such a waist but I mustn't languish over the past. Always wear blue it brings out the blue in those beautiful eyes of yours."

"Thank you. Where is Joseph?" Miriam was sure they could hear her heart beating.

"My dear, he had an arrangement to meet friends," said Rachel handing Miriam the sour milk.

Sarah added. "His head is in the clouds these days. Only talks about politics. Nothing else seems to interest him."

"Thank you Rachel. Mama will be waiting. I'd better get home," Miriam kissed Sarah and waved goodbye. She walked home slowly in the hope she might bump into Joseph. She thought about what Sarah had said and wondered if he'd said anything about them.

Avraham walked quickly, swaggering as he did so. "God, I wouldn't ask for the impossible, but I need courage to tell Becky my plans."

"Avraham I would recognize that swagger anywhere and who else is six foot around here," laughed Jacob.

"How are you today my friend?" Avraham thumped him on the back and smiled. He threw Jacob off balance as he was slight in build.

Jacob steadied himself and leaned against his horse. "So, Avraham, have you spoken to Becky about our plan yet?"

"I will, I will, soon," muttered Avraham.

"If I could loan you some courage I would my friend," said Jacob. "But, as you know I'm not too well stocked in that area myself. You should try living with a mother-in-law like Sarah," he said with a grimace.

"You'd think you had a larger burden to bear than your poor horse," and Avraham stroked the horse, trying to hide a smile. It was a straggly specimen and he could almost count the animal's ribs.

"How's Joseph doing?"

Jacob nodded. "He's a serious student and I'm proud of my son.

I can never thank you enough for making it possible."

"Just don't ever tell Becky I'm paying for Joseph to go to the Gymnasium. Makes up for our fathers who paid the Priest and we still didn't get in, remember?"

"It's not something you forget. Anyway, I won't say a word to Becky. Don't worry Avraham. I can't stop now. I'll see you on Friday night and we'll talk about our plans then." Jacob waved as he continued on his way helping his horse pull the cart uphill.

Avraham watched his friend until he disappeared over the hill looking as thin and old as his horse. Wednesday was market day in the village. Jacob sold whatever he could get his hands on. Old shoes, nails, pots, tin cans and old clothes. Peasants came from the surrounding farms, their horses pulling carts loaded with produce, pigs, seeds and some bearing the same wares as Jacob.

The following morning Becky picked up her basket and made her way to Rachel's house hitching up her skirt, and calling Miriam to follow her grumbling half under her breath.

"Your Papa is forever bumping his head. All these houses were built for midgets not for giants like your Papa, all six foot of him."

Miriam shook her head. "Papa doesn't complain so why do you?" Her thoughts turned to the lakes, rivers and forests surrounding their village where so much time had been spent with Joseph. Why wasn't he seeking her out now? Lost in thought she bumped into Joseph rushing down the path. He waved and then was gone. Why couldn't he stop and talk to her?

"Miriam, don't just stand there staring after Joseph. Can't you see it's beginning to rain? For goodness' sake, hurry up," Becky was still muttering to herself as Rachel opened the door.

"Hello Becky, come in out of the rain," and in the same breath, "Joseph can't get up in the morning, lazy that's what I told him." Brushing flour off her skirt and kneading dough for the Sabbath bread, she continued. "Would you like some tea Becky?"

Becky sat down wearily. "Yes, thank you."

"Miriam, won't you take Sarah some tea?" Rachel wiped her hands on her apron and poured the tea.

"Where's Joseph going in such a hurry?" Miriam asked. "He didn't even stop to talk to me."

Rachel winked at Becky and turned to Miriam. "He's going to meet friends. Comes back full of ideas, mostly political. I'm sure he didn't mean to be rude."

Miriam picked up the cup of tea and took it to Sarah.

Becky placed her gift on the table. "I've brought you some gooseberry preserve."

"You've a good heart, Becky. What will I do without you?"

"What do you mean? I'm not going anywhere."

"Haven't you heard? There's been another pogrom. Jacob and Avraham have been talking of nothing else and are making plans."

"I've heard about the pogrom. Who hasn't? What plans?"

"You'd better ask Avraham," said Rachel and stopped kneading. "You don't know?"

"Well, you know, so you tell me," said Becky hauling herself out of the chair.

"We're thinking of moving," whispered Rachel.

"Moving? While you're about it, you can tell me where I'm moving to?"

"Becky, don't shout. How was I to know Avraham hasn't said anything to you yet?"

"What's all the shouting about?" Sarah held onto Miriam's hand and shuffled into the kitchen.

"Becky, what's the matter? Has something happened?" asked Sarah.

Rachel turned to her mother and shook her head.

"Mama, what's wrong?" asked Miriam seeing her mother's shocked expression.

Becky swept out of the house and down the path with Miriam hurrying after her.

"Mama, what's the matter?" Miriam had to run to keep up. But her mother didn't answer. She slowed down keeping an eye open for Joseph and took her time returning home.

♣ ♣ ♣

"What's happened? Becky looks so angry." Sarah stared after Becky and Miriam.

"It's a matter between her and Avraham," said Rachel closing the front door.

"That lovely man. She's a lucky woman. I always said you should have married Avraham. We might be eating meat for Shabbat."

"Be quiet mother. I'm going to look for Jacob."

"Jacob? You'll find him sleeping beside his horse. If he worked harder he might bring meat home for supper like Avraham."

Rachel didn't answer as she turned and walked out.

♣ ♣ ♣

Avraham returned home earlier than usual warming his hands in front of the fireplace.

"Sit down Becky. There's something we need to talk about. I have a plan in mind." Avraham shifted from foot to foot.

Miriam was still thinking about Joseph as she arrived home. Something made her stop and listen at the door before going inside. She tried to take in what was being said.

"The whole town knows about a plan except me. Rachel told me, and if Sarah knows then everyone else in the village knows too."

"Just listen Becky, please. You know there's been another pogrom." He moved towards her.

Becky drew in her breath as Avraham continued. "Homes were burned, shops destroyed, families murdered and women raped. We heard that corpses were lying everywhere." He covered his face but could not hide his tears.

Becky stared at him never having seen him cry before.

"The Tzar blames the Jews for rioting and stirring up revolutionary ideas. He says we're exploiting non-Jews. Where's the evidence? If we remain here much longer, we'll either starve or die, maybe both. We must leave if we want to survive."

"But, it's time for me to arrange a marriage for Miriam."

Avraham shouted. "Do you want your daughter to be raped? Are you listening to me?"

"Don't shout and don't use that word in this house," said Becky clenching her hands.

Miriam felt tears stream down her face. Was this why Joseph was avoiding her? He hadn't wanted to tell her what a pogrom was and now she knew why. Where would they go? Would this mean being parted from Joseph? She wrapped her fingers round the little wooden heart in her pocket. The village was home and everything she knew and cared about was right here. A sob escaped as she walked towards her papa.

Avraham beckoned her to come and sit beside him. She was trembling and he put his arm around her protectively. "My child, I don't want to but we have to leave our home."

Miriam clutched the wooden heart in her hand. "Where will we go Papa?" She looked at her mama who simply shrugged her shoulders.

"I've heard good things about South Africa where we can live as free men and earn a living. A man has been going around the villages talking about the opportunities in the country. He's selling passages on a steamship to South Africa." He stopped for a moment to wipe sweat from his brow and added, "there's gold in the country." His eyes didn't leave those of Becky's. "Mr Zarinski has made an offer on my shop. Less than I wanted." He got up and paced the floor. "He knows about the pogrom in the next village and guessed I wanted a quick sale. In normal times he wouldn't be able to afford my shop."

Miriam stared at her papa. It seemed a move was inevitable.

"So, you've sold the shop?" Becky said with her hands on her hips.

"Yes, there's enough money to get us to South Africa," said Avraham. "Becky, any marriage plans for Miriam must wait. It's important we leave as soon as possible."

Miriam looked from one parent to the other. "I don't know what marriage plans Mama has but I'll decide who I wish to marry."

"Not now Miriam. Your papa and I have more urgent matters to discuss," and Becky sat down beside Avraham.

"This affects my life too. I also had plans and I've a right to know Papa's plans," said Miriam pulling up a chair and sitting down.

~ ~ ~

Miriam kept going to the window to watch out for Joseph and his family. She wore her new dress in red velvet for the photographs they were having taken later that evening. More importantly she wanted Joseph to see her looking her best.

Becky called out, "Miriam, you haven't finished setting the table. What's the matter with you? Stop going from the mirror to the window, you're making me dizzy."

Miriam broke out in a smile. "They're here," and rushed to open the door.

Becky took her apron off and kissed Rachel. "Come and sit down. Supper is ready and we must eat before we go and have photographs taken. You look good in that red dress Rachel. I don't remember seeing you ever wear it?"

Rachel replied. "It's one I wore a long time ago, but thank you. No one seems to notice what I wear these days."

Avraham winked at Becky. "What about us men? Don't we look handsome?"

Rachel took Miriam's hand. "You look lovely Miriam and red suits you."

Miriam wished it had been Joseph who said those words and went to help her mother serve the soup as both families sat down at the table. Joseph seated himself beside her father, and Miriam tried to catch his eye as she placed the soup bowls on the table almost tripping.

Becky took the soup dish out of Miriam's hand. "Watch what you're doing Miriam, you almost spilt Sarah's soup," waving her hand, "go and sit down. Rachel will help me."

Rachel stood beside Becky and whispered. "Miriam's at a difficult age Becky, and leaving everything she's ever known must be hard for her."

Becky didn't answer and waited for Avraham to say the prayers over the wine and bread. Miriam passed the bread around feeling confused as Joseph wasn't taking any notice of her.

Jacob spoke half under his breath. "I've sold our family jewellery. We had nothing else to pay for our steerage tickets."

"You did what?" said Sarah spilling soup on the tablecloth. "That jewellery belonged to Rachel's great grandmother. Your wife is the fourth generation to inherit."

Jacob grunted. "What good have your jewels ever done us? We'll all die if we stay, but maybe you'd like to wait around for the next pogrom? Rachel's great grandmother would have wanted a better life for us."

Miriam sighed seeing Sarah glaring at Jacob. She caught her mother frowning at her, but Sarah and Jacob's bickering made her feel tense.

Joseph turned to Avraham. "How'll we get to Africa?"

Avraham stirred his soup slowly before answering. "We'll head for Gdansk and board a steamship from there. It goes to England where it takes on cargo and then continues on to Africa."

"How will we get to Gdansk Papa?" asked Miriam.

Jacob answered. "We can use my horse and cart."

Sarah laughed. "Your horse can't manage one mile. May God heal his weary bones and mine," raising her eyes to heaven and mumbling. "Dear God, does Jacob plan to part the Baltic Sea next?"

Miriam couldn't help giggling and then caught her mother's eye and bit her lip.

Jacob choked on his soup. "Do you want to come with us or stay behind?"

"Jacob, be quiet," Rachel put her spoon down. "We'd end up walking if we used your horse and old cart."

Jacob raised his voice. "Did I say Sarah must walk?"

"How can you talk about leaving Sarah behind? Are you crazy?" Avraham shook his head.

"I could've told you he's crazy," said Sarah.

Avraham's fist came down hard on the table. "I'll get strong horses and a covered cart for the family. You have to sell your horse and cart Jacob."

"We must leave before Joseph's called to the Tzar's army," said Rachel.

Miriam felt a sense of dread. What if Joseph never returned as she knew had happened to so many young boys in the past.

"I could get married quickly then they won't want me in the army," laughed Joseph.

Miriam stared at Joseph. She wished he'd looked at her when he spoke about marriage. He'd hardly looked at her at all, and she was sitting beside him. She might as well have been seated beside a stone. He hadn't spoken to her since their kiss. Hadn't noticed her new dress. She tried to think what she could possibly have done to deserve his indifference, and trying to contain her resentment she blurted out. "So why don't you get married?" and saw him squirm.

"Everything has changed now Miriam. We don't know what the future holds for any of us." Joseph shrugged.

Sarah looked from Miriam to Joseph then pointed her finger at her grandson. "Wise words young man. I've seen the Jewish 'catcher' myself. They'll snatch you and we'll never see you again. I've heard mothers wailing for their sons. A terrible sound, I can tell you." She carried on slurping her soup.

Miriam noticed Jacob grimace and was beginning to wish the dinner was over.

Sarah caught Jacob looking at her in disgust. 'One day you'll also be old and have false teeth."

This time Miriam ignored her mother, caught Sarah's eye and they both laughed. For Miriam it was a release from the atmosphere around the table.

"Grandma, Tzar Alexander II stopped that law. It doesn't happen anymore," said Joseph.

"No one listens to me anymore." Sarah broke off a piece of bread and dunked it into the soup. "Such wonderful soup you make Becky. May I have some more?"

"Of course," Becky looked at Rachel. "We must plan what to take with us."

"Avraham," Rachel's voice was almost a whisper, "it's not safe to travel on our country roads."

"Don't worry, we'll keep away from the forest. I know about the armed peasants. Their fight is against the Russians not us."

Rachel replied. "I know that. But I also know they hate us."

"Why don't we just stay home," Sarah said, stifling a cough.

"I'll find out if there's a family crazy enough to have you." Jacob leant back in his chair laughing, and then said more seriously, "I'm tired of paying taxes."

"So, you think you won't pay taxes in this new country you're going to?" Sarah pointed a finger at her son-in-law.

Becky beckoned to Miriam, who stood up quickly and helped her mother pass round stewed meat and potatoes.

Miriam was glad when the dinner was over. She didn't like Jacob because of the way he spoke to Sarah. She tapped Joseph on the shoulder. "Let's go for a walk Joseph."

But her mother intervened. "Not now you two. It's time to go and have our photographs taken." Becky engineered them all out of the house. Dressed in their best clothes, Joseph and his family walked in front leaving Miriam staring at his back. She wasn't even aware of her father slipping his hand into hers. It took a long time standing before the camera. Both families were photographed separately.

Avraham hooked his arm in Becky's. "Come on Becky, you're hunched over. Anyone would think you're in mourning."

Miriam thought Rachel and family reminded her of statues. Where her father and mother had stood side by side, Joseph stood between his parents with Sarah at Rachel's side. Miriam watched as Joseph and his father stood solemnly together for a photograph. Joseph's image was imprinted on her mind forever. He looked so handsome with his newly grown beard. She thought this made him look more manly and smiled up at him. "Could we have a photograph just the two of us Joseph?"

He shifted from one foot to the other. "I'm sorry Miriam. It's a family photograph."

She turned away and was glad no one saw her tears as she wiped them on the sleeve of her new dress. The fact he didn't look at her as he spoke left her feeling uneasy.

On returning home, Jacob declared, "We'll sell everything we don't need."

"Not my bed, you hear. It's the bed in which Rachel was conceived and born."

"I'm not taking a bed on the cart. People will think you're dying."

"I'd rather die than go to a strange country. Here I have friends and what will my friend Chava do without my help?"

"Chava will have more luck, choose the right bride for the groom for a change. When was the last time you two great matchmakers were successful and made any money?" Jacob laughed. "Now, Joseph will make a good living one day. He can read and write." He slapped his son on the back.

"Grandma, I'll read the news to you if you like tonight. One day Grandma, you'll see girls will also go to school. I've been teaching Miriam to read and write."

"Yes, yes, and miracles may also happen," said Sarah. "I'm going outside for a little fresh air. I need time to think."

"Joseph, go see what's taking your grandma so long? She's been gone half an hour already., Rachel said.

Joseph did as he was told and came running inside shouting.

"What's wrong?" Rachel looked at her son's shocked face.

"It's Grandma, she's had a fall in the backyard. I need some help to get her up."

Jacob said, "Leave her there. I might be able to enjoy a little peace for a while."

"Jacob," shouted Rachel. "Go help Joseph."

When Jacob saw his mother-in-law struggling to get up, he laughed.

"Help me up you wicked man. You wish for me an early grave don't you?"

Rachel put her arm around her mother as she helped her inside. "You've scraped your knee. Let me clean it."

Sarah leaned on her daughter. "It's only a little scratch. No need to make a fuss."

Jacob shot back at Rachel, "She hasn't broken a leg. It's a scratch, that's all. Anyway, why doesn't she look where she's going?"

"I did. In fact, I have good eyes. I see a lot of things," said Sarah, shivering.

"What are you talking about old woman?" snarled Jacob.

Rachel beckoned to Jacob. "Help Mama to her room while I get some ointment for that knee. Joseph make some tea for your grandma." Whilst Joseph saw to tea, Rachel opened a kitchen cupboard and reached for the ointment.

Sarah pointed her finger at Jacob. "You're no husband for my Rachel. Why don't you take her with you when you go listen to kletzmer music? Your head's full of pretty young girls."

"What would you know? And stop pointing your finger at me." Jacob checked for Rachel out of the corner of his eye. Beads of sweat broke out on his forehead and he wiped them away with a muddied hand.

Sarah whispered in his ear. "Remember, God counts all my Rachel's tears."

Jacob turned and walked off calling out to Rachel. "I'm off to see friends."

Rachel helped Sarah onto her bed and applied the ointment. "Next time don't go outside in the dark on your own. You can't see as well as you used to. Get some rest now. I'm tired of this bickering between you and Jacob all the time."

"I'm sorry Rachel, but I have ears you know. I hear through these thin walls, and your red eyes in the mornings tell a story." Patting her daughter's hand, she lay back on the pillow and closed her eyes. "You may have a few grey hairs but you have lovely grey eyes to match and you're still slim. What more could a man want, except your husband happens to be Jacob."

"Mama, that's enough. Get some rest." Rachel passed Joseph as she hurried out of the room, blowing her nose hard and getting into a cold bed. She buried her mama's words. It was her fate and there was nothing she could do about it. She lived for Joseph now. She turned towards the wall and wiped a tear on her sleeve.

"Grandma, I've brought you some tea. You know I'll always look after you and Mama. I'll get a job when we get to Africa. You mustn't worry." He held his grandma's hand, kissing it. "I love you and Mama."

"Oh, my Joseph. Such a fine boy."

He wiped his grandma's tears away gently. "Grandma, can you show me how to dance? But what about your knee?"

Sarah took his hand. "It's a little scratch. It won't stop me from teaching my grandson to dance."

"You used to tell me, grandpa chose you because you were the best dancer." He helped her up and slowly they danced round the room.

"You must count to three for the waltz Joseph, not two. Now do that again." They carried on waltzing until Joseph could count to three. "I've got it Grandma, hooray."

"Shhh, you mustn't wake your mama." But Sarah was transported to the time she danced with her Samuel. He was so like Joseph with blue eyes and a strong jawline. Feeling slightly dizzy she sat down. "You learn quickly. Now you can teach Miriam. Such a beautiful young girl."

"It's late Grandma. I'm off to bed." He kissed her on the cheek.

Sarah said gently. "You know it'll be up to you to get a job and support the family, Joseph. Maybe you can make a good marriage?"

Joseph taking a step towards the door, paused. "I know, Grandma."

Sarah sat shaking her head. "Such responsibility for a young man to take on."

It was the Sabbath and time to go to the synagogue, a little wooden hut in the village. The two families went together. The Rabbi called them forward for a blessing.

"May God bless your journey. May you find happiness, success and safety in Africa." Then his sermon followed... "These are troubled times. We've always tried to live in peace with our neighbours. The synagogue is where we draw strength as a community. Our traditions give us courage and hope to face the future..."

The Rabbi's voice grew more distant as Avraham closed his eyes. When he looked up, the sermon was over and the community beginning to file out. He looked for Jacob. "Come on Jacob, I need to talk to you." He fumbled with his prayer book. "The ship leaves on Monday. It'll take us two days to get to the port. The first night we'll sleep at an inn. I've been told a kind lady runs the inn so we'll be safe."

Once outside, Jacob took Avraham aside. "I can't afford to pay for the whole family. Maybe Sarah could follow when I've saved enough money?"

Avraham gaped at his friend. "You can't leave Sarah behind. Who would take her in? How can you even think of such a thing? I'll help you a little."

"You're such a good friend Avraham," said Jacob as he joined his family and they all made their way home.

The next night supper was cold chicken and potatoes. Avraham, Becky and Miriam sat eating in silence. Miriam didn't much feel like talking. She touched the little wooden heart that she placed under her pillow each night. Later that night, sleep wouldn't come to her. She imagined what it would be like to marry Joseph. The home they would make together and the children she would give birth to.

But this move had changed the way things were between them. Part of her didn't want to think about it. It was enough to face leaving everything that was home to her. Eventually she felt her eyes closing but she didn't let go of the wooden heart.

THE JOURNEY

It was a cold morning as the two families set out on their journey to the coast with tickets for steerage compartments. The cart was large enough for Jacob and Avraham's families. Miriam helped her mother pack a case of clothing for each of them and a few items of sentimental value. Becky chose Sabbath candles that had been handed down from generation to generation, and Miriam placed them carefully amongst the clothing. The women handed the luggage to the men, who placed it all at the back of the cart. Avraham had bought two sturdy stallions to pull their cart and friends gathered round to say their goodbyes. Chava clutched Sarah's hand.

Salty tears spilled down Sarah's face. "I have no words my dearest Chava. Will we wander this earth and never find a safe place we can call home?"

Chava releasing her hand from Sarah's said, "Be strong for Rachel and Joseph."

Miriam's lips trembled listening to the two older women. They should have been arranging a marriage for her and Joseph. She sat silently thinking about family who had lived in the village for generations. If she felt heartbroken how much more must her mother be feeling? But still she hung on to her father, and her mother gave up her place beside Avraham and sat next to Joseph and Sarah. Jacob and Rachel sat at the back. With no time to waste, Avraham whipped the horses into action. Miriam tried to stop the flow of tears as the cart slowly made its way through the village.

The first person to speak was Jacob, who blurted out, "You still reading all that political nonsense, Joseph?"

Joseph, his voice steady, said, "You mean our literary giants? They stirred up people to bring about change, which is what I should be doing."

Sarah placed her hand gently over his. "It's better to keep out of politics, Joseph." She softly murmured the words of the writer, Julian Ursyn Niemcewicz, that she had never forgotten:

"O Exiles! Whose earthly wanderings are ne'er complete

When may you rest your sore and weary feet?

The worm has his clod of earth. The wild dove has its nest.

Everyone has a home: but the grave, for a Pole, is the only place of rest."

The journey proceeded in silence for a while, then Joseph spoke. "We can make a home anywhere, Grandma. Home is where the family is."

Sarah shrugged. "Well, we thought it was Poland once?"

Miriam whispered in her father's ear. "Joseph's right isn't he, Papa?"

Avraham looked at his daughter and nodded, pursing his lips. "That may well be, but before we feed the soul we need to feed the body. We've endured pogroms, aren't allowed outside of our towns. There's no freedom in Poland."

"You'll find freedom and peace in Heaven," muttered Jacob.

Rachel replied, her voice barely above a whisper, "Have more faith, Jacob."

Becky sat stiff and upright. "We'll find safety in Africa like Avraham said."

Avraham reached out for Miriam's hand and gave it a squeeze. They were passing the cemetery where their family were buried, and Miriam remembered listening to smatterings about her grandparents, but had never thought to ask about their lives. She felt the air was heavy with sorrow. They were leaving behind the ghosts of their ancestors whose graves they would no longer tend, nor stand beside to say a prayer of blessing. She inched nearer to her father and closed her eyes on the much loved scenes of her youth, her school and friends, knowing she would never see them or her village again. When she opened her eyes they were going through the forest that she and Joseph loved so well. She took in the Autumn hues that were a reminder of change, that nothing is constant. She thought about all the times she had sat beside Joseph, when he went fishing in the river, gleaming now as it caught the first rays of the sun. She touched the little wooden heart and glanced back at him. She caught him looking at her and she smiled, but she had the feeling they had no control over their future and it frightened her.

Her attention was distracted when, passing through the next village, she was aware of people staring at them. She averted her eyes from some of the ugly looks they were getting. "Papa, why do these people look at us like they're angry?"

Avraham touched his yamulka. "They blame us for their poverty. We've been the scapegoat throughout history. In this case it suits the Tsar to blame us for his failings." She shivered and Avraham put an arm around her.

Horrified, Miriam saw them picking up stones and next thing they were targets. She screamed. "Papa, they're throwing stones at us."

Young boys egged on by older youths were shouting. "They're Jews. Come on get them."

Joseph held onto Sarah, covering her head with a blanket, whilst Becky tried to shield herself from the larger stones. Jacob ducked and Rachel grabbed a blanket and covered her head, but not soon enough as a stone came hurtling towards her and struck her. She cried out, "My head." Touching her head her hand came away bloodied. Miriam quickly took a handkerchief from her pocket and passed it to Joseph. Her hand touched his and he nodded his thanks. Miriam saw her mother look at her intently, and she turned away. She didn't want to let on about her feelings for Joseph nor the gnawing uncertainty about his.

Avraham swore. "Those foul mouthed youth," whipping the horses and taking a detour, almost toppling the cart in his haste. When they'd left the youth safely behind them Avraham said,

"Miriam you must show people you're not afraid even if you're quivering inside."

"I can't hide my feelings, Papa. Maybe when I'm old like you." She saw her father smile and cuddled up to him. But, could she continue to hide how she felt about Joseph?

It had been unnerving and turning round, Miriam saw anxious looks on all their faces.

"Anyone hurt?" asked Avraham, keeping his eyes alert for any more trouble.

Becky replied, checking on everyone. "Rachel, you were struck. Is it bad?"

Rachel held the handkerchief to her head. "It's only a scratch Becky."

Becky pleaded, "Please go faster Avraham."

"The horses are going as fast as they can considering the load they're carrying. I can't make them go any faster." Avraham glanced up at dark clouds that were gathering.

Joseph broke the silence. "Niemcewicz was right you know. All our soldiers are used as 'cannon-fodder.'"

Sarah turned to her grandson. "You want to stay and fight for this country, you'll end up in an early grave. Now here's something you didn't learn at your Gymnasium. Your great grandparents had to be given a surname so they could be registered as a citizen."

"You're changing the subject, Grandma."

"My age allows me to say and do anything I please," she said with a nod of her head in the direction of Jacob.

"So, when was this, Grandma?"

Miriam turned to see Joseph smiling warmly at his grandmother. She cursed having to leave their village at such short notice. Hot tears ran down her cheeks and she tried not to draw attention to herself. She didn't want to listen to Joseph talking so amiably with his grandmother and tried to shut out their conversation.

Sarah's voice echoed in the forest. "Oh, sometime at the beginning of this century, a surname depended on the whim of a petty official at the Registry Office. If he had fish for dinner he would hand out the names of fishes that day. Once he received roses and handed out the names of roses. So, your great grandfather shortened his surname to Rozen."

"Do you remember what name he was given?"

"No." Sarah turned her head away, her chin up.

Joseph laughed. "Maybe the official was given some cake and roses that day and called your father Rozenkuchen."

"That's enough from you young man," said Sarah.

Miriam didn't join in the laughter. Everything had changed for her, and she couldn't blame her father and mother. Instead, she turned to Joseph hoping for a smile from him just as the cart jolted to a halt.

Avraham got up. "Jacob, take over for a while as I'm feeling rather weary." They changed places and Avraham moved to sit beside Becky and Sarah. Joseph sat next to his mother to keep an eye on her.

The road ahead was bumpy and he held onto his mother. He shouted above the noise of the wind. "Papa, be careful you're going too fast."

Jacob shouted back, "If you think you can do better take over the reins." But he remained in the driving seat.

As they moved through the villages Miriam, seated beside Jacob, was aware of his lack of concentration on the road ahead, and saw his head bend forwards and the cart jolt. He momentarily let the reins fall from his hands, making a grab for them as the horses came to an abrupt stop.

Joseph intervened. "Let me take over, Papa, you're tired."

There was no resistance from Jacob this time and he changed places with Joseph who held the reins taut on the rugged road. Miriam saw him glance at her and couldn't help giving him a look of entreaty.

Joseph leant over and whispered, "Miriam, I will have to take care of my family now. You must be strong for your mama and papa."

"What are you saying Joseph?" She looked at him puzzled

unsure whether there was another meaning to his words.

Just then they rounded a corner and before Joseph could answer Avraham said, "I think this is a good spot for lunch Joseph, and we can all do with stretching our legs. The horses also need food and a rest."

Rachel and Becky spread a blanket on the grass. They sat shaded by trees. Miriam felt bathed by the silence of the forest, with only the sounds of nature to disturb the peace. She felt as if she was floating, watching the leaves fall to the ground, and breathing fresh air as if God's breath was upon her face. They had prepared food for the journey and everyone was hungry despite feeling tired. There was blinchiki with cheese and Avraham's favourite, a sour milk drink.

Sarah placed a blinchiki on a plate and gave it to Rachel who picked at her food. "You must eat something my child."

Jacob turned round sharply to face Sarah. "Rachel isn't a child. You're turning into a senile old woman."

Becky turned on Jacob. "We're all upset having to leave our homeland, Jacob. Don't take it out on Sarah. She means well."

They ate in silence and Joseph went to feed the horses and give them water.

Miriam leaned against her mother who noticed her white face. "What's the matter Miriam?"

Miriam jumped up and ran to the lake's edge, where she vomited. Joseph ran after her, and helped her back to the cart covering her with a blanket.

"Joseph, I'm upset, not ill." She was aware everyone was listening and said no more, covering herself with the blanket.

They resumed the journey and Joseph climbed into the cart beside Miriam and kissed her hand. He whispered, "I'm sorry, Miriam. Maybe things might have been different if we'd stayed in our village. Call it fate if you like."

"Things? What things? I don't understand what you mean?" Tears were not far away. Miriam raised her voice and didn't hold back. "Well, let fate decide your life then. I'll decide my own destiny," and turned away from him.

Joseph merely shrugged and pulled on the reins causing the horses to pick up speed.

No one spoke except Avraham. "You're tired Joseph let me take the reins and we'll make for the inn where we can all have a rest." He patted Miriam's hand as he took his place beside her.

The wind was stronger now and the horses were kicking up dust as they were driven forwards at a fast pace.

"We need to get to the inn before dark," said Avraham.

"Thank goodness you're a practical man, organising everything for us," Becky said with a sigh touching Avraham gently on the shoulder.

"And how come I get such praise, long overdue I might add?" Avraham let out a guffaw.

Becky leaned forward and whispered in his ear. "Joseph's a responsible lad. He'd make a good husband." She looked at her daughter who had closed her eyes.

"Joseph will need to be even more responsible when we get to Africa," whispered Avraham.. "He'll have to get a job to support his family and find a bride with a wealthy papa."

Miriam pretended not to hear her father and felt a sense of foreboding. She turned to look at Joseph but he was gazing into the distance.

Avraham shouted, "I can see the inn. We'll stop here for the night. It's been a very long day for us and the horses."

It was already dark and the lights inside looked inviting. Yet all Miriam could think about was Joseph. Inwardly she was in a dark place as they made their way towards the entrance of the inn.

THE INN

Miriam heard the inn keeper remark how wise they were to use a Haflinger to pull their cart. She watched her father being lead away to take care of the horses and all the while she had one eye on

Joseph. They were ushered to an alcove where there was a long table and benches to sit on. Becky made her stay with the others and went to look for Avraham. The fire was well stoked and Miriam closed her eyes to the hum of people talking, breathing in the aroma of burning wood that reminded her of home. She blinked on opening her eyes. It was dark with candles the only source of light in the room.

"It doesn't feel safe here," murmured Sarah looking at the men in the inn. "Do we have to sleep here?"

"Just be grateful we have a roof over our heads. If it's not good enough for you, sleep in the cart," said Jacob.

The inn keeper placed a dish of food on the table and a jug of ale, Sarah tasted the stew. "It's overcooked," and pulled a face pushing her plate away.

"No, it's not. I'll eat it if you don't want it." Jacob didn't hesitate to help himself to her portion.

"Grandma, you'll go hungry. You should try and eat a little."

"It's too late now, your papa has gobbled it all up."

Jacob downed his ale in one gulp. "Joseph, go and see what's keeping Avraham and Becky before their food gets cold."

"How can you send a young boy? Look at those rough men," whispered Rachel.

Miriam moved nearer to Sarah and away from a young man ogling her. When he smiled she noticed he had teeth missing. His hair was long and straggly but it was his eyes that bothered her the most. He stared with a leering look. She shivered and looked away.

Sarah called the inn keeper over. "Do you have any chicken?"

"Anything wrong with the meat?" asked the inn keeper.

"The stew is not to my taste," Sarah didn't mince her words. "It's tough. You see some of my teeth are loose." She opened her mouth to show him.

"Well, what would you like?" asked the inn keeper, refraining from smiling.

"I would like, as you're asking, some soup and chicken."

Miriam giggled at Jacob staring open-mouthed at his mother-in-law and was certain she saw a twinkle in the inn keeper's eye. He certainly looked like he enjoyed his food and wasn't fussy like Sarah, and carried his weight well as he was tall. Most of all she liked his cheerful manner.

"That's quite an order. You must be very hungry, in which case I'll see if I can satisfy you. Come with me," and helped Sarah to her feet.

"Mother, I'll go with you," said Rachel turning on Jacob as he got up to follow them. "Jacob how can you think of leaving Miriam on her own. Miriam, come my child."

Miriam relieved to get away from "ogling eyes" felt irked being referred to as a "'child." Would they never stop calling her a child?

The inn keeper led them to the kitchen. "Meet my wife, Ruth, and I'm Maurice," gesturing with his hands for them to sit down.

Sarah sat down at the table with Miriam and they watched Ruth at work. Soon the women were exchanging recipes and eating soup and chicken. Miriam looked at Sarah when Jacob told Maurice that he had organised everything for their journey. Miriam rolled her eyes at Sarah who was looking like she could blow a fuse.

Joseph and Becky found Avraham asleep in the barn. "Look what you're doing to your best coat," said Becky brushing hay off and waking Avraham.

"Leave me alone, woman," he mumbled, struggling to his feet. Joseph gave him a hand and they walked back to the inn where Maurice was waiting. He led them into the kitchen and Avraham turned to his Host. "Thank you for your hospitality."

"No need, Mr Levensky. I've heard you have a long journey ahead of you. Ruth will take you to your rooms after you've had something to eat. Come and join us for an ale later when the inn is quiet if you're not too tired."

Miriam didn't mind sharing a room with Sarah and looked out of the window. "It's cold in here Sarah."

"The room is clean so don't complain," said Sarah.

Miriam followed the road with its poplars swaying in the gentle breeze. It was another image to remember. It felt like a series of goodbyes. Each moment sealed in time and her memory. She drew the heavy curtains closed and got into bed, pretending to fall asleep. The strangeness of the surroundings made her shiver rather than the cold, and the unknown that lay before her. She felt as if she was being swallowed up by an uncertain future.

Later that evening, the men, Rachel and Becky sat around a roaring fire with glasses of ale for the men and tea for the women. It was a sparsely furnished room saved from austerity by a few comfortable chairs in which Avraham was now seated nearest the fire warming his hands, whilst Maurice and Joseph talked softly. Avraham turned towards them catching their last words and mulling them over as he drank the ale.

"Alexander III introduced an anti-Jewish policy," Maurice said. "You're wise to leave the country now."

"I know," replied Joseph, "what's more he believes Jewish intellectuals are stirring up revolutionary ideas."

"We hope to make a better life for ourselves in South Africa," said Avraham.

Maurice nodded and lowered his voice. "We heard about the pogrom. There's no future for our children, but it's too late for me and Ruth. We're too old and tired." He filled their glasses and raised his own. "May God walk with you," to which they all drank deeply.

Rachel saw a smile on her husband's face as he snored softly. She left him sleeping in the chair as she and Becky said goodnight and went up to their rooms.

Maurice collected the glasses and tea cups. "I'd just leave him be. Let Jacob sleep off the ale. The fire will keep him warm during the night," and said goodnight to Avraham and Joseph as they headed to their rooms.

Miriam tossed and turned whilst she slept. The cold woke her and she sat up holding her head in her hands.

"What is it Miriam?" said Sarah half awake.

"I dreamt I saw Joseph getting married."

"Well, one day you and Joseph will get married."

"No, no. You don't understand. It wasn't me he was marrying. This woman, she had her back to me and I couldn't see her face. Mama and Papa weren't there so how could it be me? It was so cold and the noise of the wind was eerie. Sarah, the wind was howling and telling me someone was dying and that was me because I was losing Joseph. Don't you see Sarah, it was like death to me."

"It's only a dream my child. Hush now, you must get some sleep."

But Miriam couldn't sleep. The dream was an omen. With a pillow wet with tears she couldn't shake off her feeling of foreboding. Eventually Sarah's faint snores lulled her to sleep.

GDANSK

The men talked quietly whilst Miriam watched the sun come up and hope fill the sky. She sat beside Joseph who held the reins on the last leg of the journey to the port of Gdansk. She wouldn't have minded if their journey had gone on forever. The air was crisp and she tugged at her skirt that kept shifting in the wind.

Sarah sat with hunched shoulders, murmuring almost to herself. "Maybe I should go back now whilst I can. You have to be stoical to make a new life."

"Too late now and you were the one who said we shouldn't look back. We don't have far to go now, Sarah," said Avraham.

"Since when have you been a philosopher, Sarah?" sneered Jacob.

Avraham looked askance at Jacob. "We'd do well to follow Sarah's advice if we're to survive in Africa."

Becky bowed her head as if in prayer.

"So, is there a God after all?" Avraham eyed his wife quizzically.

Becky sighed, "I wish we were near the port."

"Well, your prayer has been answered." Avraham raised his hand, pointing at a signpost to Gdansk.

Miriam inhaled sea air as they rounded a corner and entered the harbour area. In the chaos of a crowded dock with people arriving in horse and carts to board the ship, her father found a horse trader willing to barter. The horse trader growled as he examined the horses, "These horses aren't worth what you're asking."

"They may be tired but you can see they're strong animals, and it's a solid cart." Avraham stood his ground. When the man gave his final offer Avraham accepted. He pocketed the money and they walked towards the ship. People kept bumping into him on the way and Miriam hung on to her father.

"Watch where you're going," shouted Avraham above the din and activity going on all around them. Once on board, he checked his pocket.

Miriam saw the look on his face. "Is something wrong Papa?" He shook his head. But she saw him fumbling in his pocket and guessed the reason. "Papa, we'll manage," knowing only too well how her mama would react.

After boarding and depositing the trunks in their cabins, Miriam knocked on the door of Joseph's cabin. "I'm going to take a walk round the deck. Do you want to come with me, Joseph?"

Soon they were both leaning over the railings excitedly and looking out onto a scene of great activity. Men were loading all manner of goods onto the ship. People were clambering up the gangway carrying large suitcases. Orders were being shouted and amidst the chaos Miriam noticed a young woman board, her blonde hair held in place by a bonnet. She wore a long emerald green dress such as Miriam had never seen before. She turned to speak to Joseph unaware he was no longer at her side. When she turned back she was astonished to see him at the young woman's side carrying her trunk. They were talking as they approached her.

"Miriam, this is Hannah. I could see she was struggling with a heavy trunk and had to go to her aid."

Miriam held out her hand but she was looking at the way Joseph's eyes never left Hannah's face. She took an instant dislike to Hannah.

As the days passed at sea she hardly saw Joseph and whenever she did he was at Hannah's side. Hannah was arousing feelings that she'd never had before. She watched Hannah flirt with Joseph. Watched Hannah stumble on deck and Joseph putting his hand out to steady her, and Hannah cosying up to him. It made her want to shove Hannah from behind so she would really trip up. Wily, that's what Hannah was, thought Miriam.

Whilst eating dinner in the dining room they listened to Hannah telling them about her uncle who had a textile business in England, and was slowly bringing out family to join him because he needed staff he could trust. As far as Miriam was concerned, Hannah couldn't be trusted. She believed Hannah was embellishing her story by saying how her uncle wanted her to come and help look after his children because his wife had died recently. Everyone thought she was so brave to be travelling on her own, and it annoyed Miriam that Joseph seemed to be taken in by whatever Hannah told them.

Miriam rose early one morning, knocking on Joseph's cabin. He opened the door still half asleep. "Joseph, will you join me for a walk around the deck?"

Joseph yawned. "Miriam, it's too early. I was up late last night. Maybe another day."

"What's the matter Joseph? We've hardly spent any time together. We used to share everything, and now you don't have time to talk to me?"

"I'm sorry if you're upset, Miriam. We'll talk but another time. Right now, I'm tired and must get some sleep," and he closed the door.

Miriam paced up and down the corridor until she saw Hannah coming towards her. She turned her back on Hannah and headed down the corridor, stopping at the end to look back and watched Hannah knocking on Joseph's cabin. The door opened and Hannah went in. Miriam felt frustrated as she knew she would never have been allowed to be alone with Joseph in his cabin. Besides, suddenly Joseph wasn't tired anymore? The journey was beginning to feel interminable and she waited for an opportunity to get Joseph alone but Hannah was always at his side.

One morning Miriam bumped into Hannah and Joseph.

Hannah greeted her with the sweetest of smiles. "Do you want to join us Miriam? We're going up for breakfast."

Miriam fixed her eyes on Joseph. "Yes, I'd love to." She couldn't help noticing Joseph slipping his hand out of Hannah's. She was like a snake curling herself around Joseph. She didn't listen to Hannah's constant chatter, instead her eyes bored into Joseph's back as he walked ahead of them. She felt her world was turning grey like the sky and the sea outside. Today she'd looked out of the cabin window and seen waves so high she was afraid the ship would sink. Food stuck in her throat watching Joseph and Hannah talking and laughing. She managed to wedge herself in between them at breakfast. But it was as if she wasn't there for all the notice Joseph took of her, and Hannah didn't give her a chance to talk.

"Miriam, you must eat something," Becky implored her, having joined their table.

"It's Sarah who's not eating. Leave me alone. I'm not a child." She pushed her chair back from the table, cast a last look at Joseph and marched off to her cabin. Feeling claustrophobic and bored in the cabin she decided to take a walk along the deck, but the wind was so strong that the door slammed behind her on the deck. Deck chairs were piled one on top of the other so they didn't get blown out to sea. Waves were being whipped up by the wind but the smell of sea air made her feel she could breathe. She certainly couldn't breathe seated next to Hannah and the way Joseph looked at her. Beginning to feel nauseous from the rolling of the ship she retraced her steps and went indoors passing the lounge where a few people were playing cards. She went past the dining room but couldn't see any sign of Joseph or Hannah and headed down the stairs back to her cabin with a bitter taste in her mouth.

♣ ♣ ♣

Sarah wasn't feeling well and had been laid up in bed for most of the trip. The heaving of the ship was too much for her, and she was nauseous. It fell to Miriam to look after her as she was sharing a cabin with Sarah.

"Shall I get the doctor for you?" Miriam looked at Sarah's pasty colour, and noticed Sarah seemed to have difficulty breathing.

"No, no. I'm just a little seasick."

She passed the time reading to Sarah even though it was hard to concentrate.

"You've already read that page Miriam. Maybe you need glasses?"

"Sorry, I need some air. I'll look in on you later." She was restless, unable to be still for a second thinking about what Hannah and Joseph might be doing in his cabin. She couldn't sit beside Sarah when she needed to be near Joseph distracting him from the attentions of Hannah. "Maybe I should get the doctor for you Sarah. Or I could fetch Joseph to come and keep you company."

"How many times do I have to tell you I don't want to see a doctor and what can Joseph do? Miriam, you're the one who needs a doctor. Look at you fading away. Don't think I haven't noticed. You're not eating, and keeping me awake with your nightmares."

"What nightmares?"

"I can't sleep because you keep crying out at night."

Miriam couldn't remember a time when she and Sarah had cross words but now she was just anxious to go.

"Why are you saying these things?"

"Because I know what's behind it all," said Sarah.

Miriam couldn't stop the tears. She'd held them at bay for so long. Sarah put her arm around her and waited until she composed herself.

"It's Joseph," said Miriam. "He doesn't have time to talk to me anymore."

"I know you love him, but you're still very young. Perhaps it's not God's plan for you."

"God's plan for me? What about my plans. I want Joseph."

"It may not be Joseph's plan," said Sarah shaking her head.

Miriam got up and stood in front of the mirror. She undid her bun and let her long black hair cascade over her shoulders and down her back. "Aren't I as pretty as Hannah?"

"Miriam, you're beautiful. You'll have many suitors in the future."

"Why don't you listen to me? I don't want other suitors. I want Joseph," and walked out slamming the door behind her.

The next day there was an announcement. They were to dock in England the following day and the captain invited everyone to a dinner and dance that evening. Miriam put on her best dress and admired herself in the mirror. The gown was nipped in at the waist and she loved the soft red velvet material. She did a twirl and put some lipstick on and earrings her mother had given her. She thought she looked more sophisticated having lost some of her roundness and this would surely get Joseph's attention. She was nervous but at the same time excited that Joseph would surely notice how grown up she looked, and want to dance with her and not Hannah.

Dinner was a mutton stew and dessert was pastries served with tea. Before they took their seats Joseph gave Miriam a kiss on the cheek and said, "You look lovely tonight, Miriam."

She smiled up at him and felt flushed and happy to sit beside Joseph. When Hannah tried to make conversation, Miriam interrupted her as if she hadn't heard, ignoring Joseph's look of annoyance.

It was over dinner that Rachel disclosed their altered plans. "Hannah has told Joseph she is sure her uncle will have a job for him at his factory, so we'll be disembarking in London." She added, "Another week on board ship would be just too much for Sarah."

Miriam sat shocked, almost unable to breathe. Hannah had got her way with Joseph. She hated Hannah. She saw Hannah's hand on Joseph's thigh. Felt her world crumbling. Why hadn't she claimed Joseph in the way she was sure Hannah had. The times she'd seen Hannah go into his cabin. She cursed Hannah silently, forming words that hadn't passed her lips before. The band struck up a waltz and to her dismay, Joseph held out his hand to Hannah and she watched them move onto the dance floor.

"Come, Miriam. I can still do the waltz," Avraham held his hand out to his daughter.

"Papa, I need fresh air." She felt in a daze almost tripping on her long dress as she ran up the stairs to the deck. She stood holding onto the railings watching the waves break against the ship's side. She felt a pull towards the sea below her. It would be so easy to end this pain. She heard her name – was it the sea calling to her? Then felt a tap on her shoulder and turned round. It was Hannah.

"I've wanted to talk to you for some time, Miriam. Do you mind if I join you?"

Miriam stared at her, barely taking in what she was saying.

"Miriam, you know Joseph so well. He says you've grown up together and become close friends. I thought he might have spoken to you about us."

"I haven't seen much of Joseph on this trip," Miriam replied, her voice barely above a whisper.

"I thought he might have mentioned his intentions to you."

"Intentions?" she could barely talk, gritting her teeth.

"Well, that we're engaged. We're going to announce it tonight."

Miriam stared at Hannah unable to speak, wanting to spit out the anger and hatred she was feeling towards her.

"Oh, you poor thing, you must be so cold standing here without your shawl. Come below and have some wine with us to celebrate."

Miriam acted on impulse pushing Hannah against the railings as she fled. Bumping into people she ran downstairs to the cabin and flung herself on the bed wishing she had answered the call of the sea.

♣ ♣ ♣

The captain raised his glass and announced in a gruff voice. "If I can have your attention for a brief moment. We have a couple who've become engaged on board ship, and I wish to toast them as I'm sure we all do. May you both be very happy together."

Joseph turned to Hannah. "Where's Miriam?"

Hannah spoke quietly. "I told her about us and I think she's upset."

"I should have told her myself," said Joseph.

Sarah left the party with Avraham and Becky. "I'll speak to her, Becky. Leave her to me. You know how close we are and Miriam confides in me."

Back in the cabin, Sarah wrapped her arms around Miriam. "Joseph is doing what he has to, providing for the family. It's an opportunity he can't turn down."

Miriam's words came between sobs. "He'll have opportunities in Africa. He could get a job in Africa. He doesn't have to marry Hannah to get a job."

During the night Miriam was unable to sleep not knowing how she was going to get through the next day.

The following morning Jacob's family were ready to disembark together with Hannah. Avraham, Becky and Miriam stood on deck and bade them a tearful farewell. It had taken all of Miriam's strength to join her parents and she couldn't look at Joseph for fear of crying.

Avraham turned to Rachel, "Here's the address where we'll be staying in South Africa. Write and let us know how you're all settling down."

Rachel embraced Avraham then Becky and Miriam. "I'll miss you all so much," she said with her voice breaking.

Jacob shook hands with Avraham and grasped Becky's hand, unable to speak.

Sarah turned to Miriam. "You've been like a granddaughter to me. You must be strong for your Mama and Papa. God has other plans for you."

Miriam couldn't speak. Not only was she losing Joseph but Sarah as well.

Joseph came towards her. "I'll miss you Miriam my dearest friend. We have such happy memories of growing up together. I'll never forget you," and wrapping her in his arms he kissed her wet cheeks.

She reached for his hands and whispered in desperation. "I thought there was something between us."

Just then Hannah called to him. "Joseph, I can see my uncle. He's waiting for us."

"I'm coming Hannah. Just need a few words with Miriam. I couldn't promise you anything Miriam. You do understand I have to look after my family." His cheek wet with Miriam's tears, he turned and strode towards Hannah.

Avraham put his arm around her as she cried unashamedly watching Joseph disappearing down the gangway.

Miriam put up with her father hovering over her for the rest of the voyage. She was never left alone. Her mother moved into the cabin with her and Miriam didn't object. It didn't help that the seas were rough and they couldn't take a walk on the deck. She felt claustrophobic but the heartache was the worst. She just wanted the journey to end.

When finally they heard the captain announce their arrival in Cape Town they went up on deck. Miriam looked out on what seemed to her a majestic mountain covered in cloud. The sun shone and its warmth permeated her.

Avraham hugged her. "The African sun is called the poor man's blanket, did you know that, Miriam?"

She smiled for a brief moment and watched women in long gowns and pretty bonnets walking along the pier as they docked. There were also people in rowing boats enjoying an outing.

Her voice was barely a whisper. "Papa, I saw this mountain in a dream."

THE CAPE OF GOOD HOPE

The family disembarked and Avraham looked around for a contact. He had on his yarmulka. He had been told they would be met when the ship docked in the harbour. He noticed a group of men standing to one side. One of the men came up and introduced himself.

"The name's Monty Herman. You are..." and looked at a piece of paper he was holding, "Avraham Levensky?"

"Yes. Pleased to meet you Mr Herman, and this is my wife and daughter." The men shook hands.

"Just call me Monty and welcome to your new country. He nodded in the direction of Becky and Miriam. "Had a good journey did you?" Without waiting for an answer he continued. "Follow me. I'll get you through immigration quicker."

The family followed Monty as he pushed his way as far forward as the multitude of people would allow. Miriam looked around. Everything looked grey but then her whole world felt "grey" to her. Grief wrapped itself around her and she longed to be left alone and not have her mother hanging around her all the time, as though she was about to do something foolish like throw herself overboard whilst they were on the ship. Her mother hadn't let her out of her sight and she felt claustrophobic. Freeing herself from her mother's grip she stood beside her father.

Eventually they made it to the desk where an official peered over the rim of his glasses at them. "Your name please."

Monty coughed and whispered in Avraham's ear, "Shorten your name. It'll make life easier for you and the family. Lots of men do it."

"Name please," said the official, frowning as he looked over his glasses at Avraham. The official's voice reverberated around the room and Avraham hesitated.

Monty whispered. "Just say Leven. It's not dishonourable to change your name, it's practical."

Avraham uttered the name, "Leven, Sir."

They walked back to where their belongings had been loaded onto a cart. Miriam was silent, taking in the new surroundings and listening to the men talk. Without further ado they were taken to a boarding house, an arrangement organised by the community. They passed the Gardens Synagogue which Monty pointed out.

"You can walk from your boarding house to the synagogue. Why don't you come to the service tonight and meet the community. I want you to meet my wife, Esther, and you must have supper with us after the service."

Avraham prodded by Becky answered. "Thank you, that's most kind."

The boarding house was situated in Government Avenue. Wood furniture dominated the interior of their flat which had two bedrooms, a small lounge, bathroom and a tiny kitchen. Miriam thought it was warm and homely. Most of all she liked the window in the lounge that looked out onto a tree lined avenue.

"Papa, there are black slaves working here," exclaimed Miriam, spotting some cleaners as she peered out of the window.

"They aren't slaves although once they were, so I was told. They came from East Africa, Madagascar and the East Indies some-where around 1652 and were freed in 1838 when Britain occupied this land."

"Free to do menial work. That's not freedom, Papa."

"So, we have a philosopher in our midst," he looked at his daughter with a twinkle in his eye.

"I didn't know you knew so much about the country," said Becky, looking up from her unpacking.

"I got talking to an officer on the ship. He also told me that the gold fields are far from the Cape, at least a thousand miles." Becky nodded, preoccupied sorting out their clothes.

That evening they walked to the synagogue. It was not far and Miriam looked at the mountain she had dreamed about towering in front of them. A cloud hovered over the top and soon covered it.

"Papa, do you believe in God?"

"No, my child."

"Then why go to the synagogue?"

"Well, it's always been a meeting place, and where I hope we'll make new friends."

"Papa, don't you think it's strange that I dreamed about the mountain?"

"I dream about finding gold," he said winking at Becky who gripped his hand and made him slow down so they were a little way behind Miriam.

Becky whispered., "Maybe losing Joseph to Hannah has unhinged Miriam. I worry about her."

"You're a worrier, Becky. They're only dreams. She'll get over Joseph as soon as she meets another young man."

They walked on in silence whilst Miriam struggled to keep her skirt from flying up in the southeaster wind.

It was Friday night and the synagogue was full. Miriam sat upstairs with her mother separated from the men who sat downstairs. The service seemed to go on forever. She was bored and stifled a yawn.

"I'm starving. How much longer is this service?" The choir's singing masked the rumbling noises her stomach was making.

"Shh," whispered Becky. "Soon, I hope. It's been a very long day and I'm also tired."

Monty sat next to Avraham and after the service introduced him to a few of the congregants and the Rabbi. When he saw Esther he called out to her, "Stop talking woman and come meet Avraham and his family."

After introductions they travelled in Monty's carriage to his house overlooking a dam and the town below. A grand house with many rooms, a courtyard and raised garden situated on a steep slope leading up to the mountain behind it.

Esther took Miriam's hand. "If you walk to the top of our mountain, you will have the most wonderful view of the mountains and sea. Perhaps my son, David, can take you up sometime," and immediately called out, "David, come and meet our guests".

David made his appearance at the same time as a black woman bearing a soup tureen. His warm smile put Miriam at her ease and he looked about her age. He was just about to open his mouth when his mother said, "Shh David."

Monty began supper with a blessing, "May God bless us and may you and your family, Avraham, settle down in your new country, amen," and indicated they should all sit.

The meal commenced with homemade chicken soup.

"So, what do you do David?" asked Avraham.

"I help Pa in his shop but I'd like to be a doctor one day."

"A fine goal young man."

Miriam concentrated on the food. One course after another until she felt she couldn't swallow another morsel. She half listened to her father describing their journey from the Shtetl. She wanted to shut it out. Obliterate every image that remained of Joseph. She was relieved when the meal came to an end.

Avraham followed Monty to his study. The study was a room encircled by wood panelling with hundreds of books lining its shelves. Monty eyed Avraham and pre-empted his questioning look. "I'm a self-educated man. You learn a great deal about the world through books. I never had much schooling, too poor. Came up the hard way. Opened a shop and thank God it's well supported by farmers who come from miles around."

"What do you sell?"

"Saddles, medicines, coffee, tea, agricultural implements – a little of this and a little of that. You must come and see. But now tell me, what are your plans?"

Avraham sank into an old armchair fingering his beard. "I thought of prospecting for gold."

Monty poured him a glass of brandy which he raised in a toast. "To your success on the goldfields and to everyone's health."

Avraham swallowed the brandy.

"Look, why don't you come and work for me until you and the family are settled?"

"That's a very generous offer, but I can't accept charity, and the community have already provided us with a place to stay." Avraham shifted in the armchair.

"Nonsense. I expect you to work very hard for your money, and you'll be paying rent as soon as you're working." Monty refilled Avraham's glass.

Miriam sat on the verandah with David and watched the servant disappear into the house.

"Have you always had a servant?"

David laughed. "Thabisa practically brought me up. Her name means to bring joy. When I was a baby she carried me wrapped in a blanket on her back whilst she cleaned the house. It's the custom in Africa."

"What a beautiful name but where was your mama?"

"Helping my pa in the shop. But tell me about your life in the Schtetl. That's where you come from, isn't it?"

Miriam paused, before speaking softly so David had to lean forward to hear her. She didn't know where to begin. Her life had been so different. How could she describe how they had lived to David who lived in such grandiose surroundings with a servant who did everything for him? She took a deep breath. "We had a wooden house in the Schtetl, and were a close community living next door to each other. We kept a cow and hens in the backyard." Talking about home was making her homesick and thinking of Joseph, she paused. "I had a close friend who taught me to read and write." She closed her eyes as if it could bring back the past.

Waiting until she opened her eyes, David asked, "It must be so hard to leave your home and everyone you grew up with." When

Miriam didn't answer he asked, "Would you like me to show you around the town sometime?"

Miriam didn't have a chance to reply as Monty appeared and said it was time to take them home. The horse and cart took off with Esther imploring Becky to visit soon.

"Such a good looking young man, isn't he Miriam? And he wants to be a doctor," said Becky emphasising the word doctor.

Miriam looked away.

One evening whilst Becky and Miriam were washing up, Avraham blurted out. "Becky, I've decided it's time to go to the goldfields."

Miriam looked at her mother's angry face and escaped to the bedroom. She could hear their raised voices through the thin wall, and paced the room listening to her mother shouting.

"You bring us to a new country and then desert us. You expect me to work and put bread on the table while you go searching for gold you may never find. I suppose you want Miriam and me to work in Monty's shop?"

Avraham replied, "I've had a generous offer from Monty for you and Miriam to take my place in the shop. I've made up my mind and that's that. Work is the best antidote for Miriam and will be for you too whilst I'm gone."

"And how long do you expect to be gone?"

"I don't know. However long it takes, and for goodness' sake keep your voice down, everyone in this building can hear you."

Miriam heard her father's footsteps pass her room and felt a knot in her stomach as she thought of them being left on their own. She loved her papa and knew he would never desert them. When all was quiet Miriam fell into a fitful sleep.

The following day Avraham took them to see Monty's shop. Miriam was acutely aware of the silence between her parents. They walked past people selling their wares at market stalls, all manner of goods as Saturday was market day in the town.

"The fish smells awful Papa. Do we have to walk this way?" Miriam wrinkled up her nose in disgust, and got no answer from her father. They passed a meat stall with carcasses hanging up to dry. She picked up her skirts to avoid bits of raw meat the butcher had thrown on the ground for his dog. It was a relief when she saw the flower market. "Oh, look at those flowers, what are they?"

"Miss, these are proteas. A penny each," said the flower seller.

"No thank you," replied Becky taking Miriam's hand. "We've got to keep up with your papa otherwise we'll get lost." They picked up pace to catch up with Avraham who was striding ahead.

Miriam breathed in the scent of brightly coloured roses as they walked past. "Papa do you have to walk so fast? How much is a penny worth in zlotys?"

"You have to learn about pounds and pence now and forget about zlotys." Avraham pointed, "Look there's the castle. It served as both a prison as well as a fort."

Miriam was glad when her papa finally slowed down as they came to a district thronging with life. They continued walking along the main street with shops on either side. Carts passed them laden with goods. She felt hot and sweaty with the African sun bearing down on them and squinted in the strong sunlight. A young man was loading his cart as they arrived at Monty's shop. Monty was standing outside talking and drew Avraham aside.

"Let me introduce you to one of our best customers, Dirk Uys. A successful farmer from Elgin." The men shook hands.

"I believe you want to travel to the goldfields. I know a Mr van Jaarsveld who organises transport," said Dirk. "Mr van Jaarsveld sets off each Monday at precisely twelve noon. You mustn't be late. As soon as the noon gun goes off from Signal Hill the wagon departs."

"Thank you, Mr Uys."

"Please call me Dirk."

Miriam turned away embarrassed by his stare. She was relieved when the men went into Monty's office to talk and she and her mother could look around the shop.

"A fine shop, Miriam. Look at all these goods," Becky whispered. "Monty must be a wealthy man. Perhaps it won't be so bad working here."

Shelves were bursting with saddles stacked on top of each other in different sizes. Agricultural implements took up half the shop floor. Coffee, tea and biscuits were behind a counter where David stood putting together a parcel for Dirk and waved to Miriam.

"Hello, it's good to see you. Would you like me to show you around Miriam?"

"Hello David, that would be very kind of you, wouldn't it Miriam? I'll just wait here to speak to your pa." Becky smiled at David and sat down on a chair that she first dusted off with her hand.

Monty slapped Dirk on the back. "Be careful now with that load on your cart."

Dirk turned to Becky. "May I call on your daughter?"

Becky looked to Avraham, and Dirk looked from one to the other finally addressing Avraham. "May I call on your daughter?"

Before Avraham could answer Monty interrupted. "Ah, young man so you want to take out Becky and Avraham's beautiful daughter."

"Certainly you may," interrupted Avraham giving Dirk their address without looking at Becky.

Miriam stood beside David embarrassed especially as Dirk had asked in the presence of everyone. She could feel everyone's eyes on her and hardly dared breathe. What was her father thinking? They knew nothing about Mr Uys other than he was a farmer. Feeling awkward she didn't care whether she saw Dirk Uys or not, and put it out of her mind when they returned home.

Later that evening Becky turned to Avraham when they were in their bedroom. "Dirk is an Afrikaner, he's Christian Avraham. Why are you encouraging him?"

"Afrikaners go by the Old Testament same as us. I don't know why you're so worried. It'll be good for Miriam and take her mind off Joseph."

Becky shook her head. "You can be naïve sometimes. You would never have agreed to this in the Shtetl."

"Yes well, we're not in the Shtetl anymore. I don't want to discuss this anymore. I'm tired."

"All you can think about is going to find gold."

Miriam wrapped the blanket over her ears to erase their voices, and wished she could erase some of her memories at the same time.

JANUARY 1887

THE GOLDFIELDS

Avraham made his way towards the passenger wagon carrying a small bag with a few belongings. He left Becky promising to write as soon as he arrived at the goldfields. There were tearful good-byes. Becky clinging to him so he had to gently disengage himself. His Becky who had always seemed so strong and independent. He kissed Miriam, "Look after your mama."

Miriam tried to smile through her tears. "We'll manage, Papa. You mustn't worry about Mama. I'll look after her."

"You make me feel proud Miriam. It's hard to leave you and your mama behind." He waved and they lost sight of him in the throng of people walking down the tree lined avenue.

Avraham arrived as the noon gun went off.

"Thought you wouldn't make it, Mr Leven. Climb aboard," said Mr van Jaarsveld.

The wagon moved forward with a jolt. There were half a dozen men smoking and talking about their previous exploits. He listened as they discussed having to leave their jobs, going back and forth prospecting for gold. Two of the men spoke a language foreign to him.

"It's Afrikaans," said one of the men observing Avraham. "Is this your first time prospecting?" to which Avraham nodded. "It won't be your last. You get hooked and can't stop once you start. I've heard of plenty success stories." He took a puff on his pipe. I'm Piet Potgieter, farmer by trade from Elgin. Glad to meet you."

Avraham looked at him puzzled. "Why are you going prospecting when you have a farm?"

"Same as everyone else. If I find gold I can buy more cattle."

Avraham estimated Piet must be a good twenty years younger than himself. There was a camaraderie amongst the men and soon he was at ease in their company. He sat back and listened to an Englishman claiming to have been a magician and actor in England before arriving in the Cape. This was his second trip to the Rand.

"Name is Michael McKay, well that was my stage name. Shakespeare, that's what I acted in." He talked incessantly until Avraham felt himself nodding off to the man's monotonous drone. Seemed to him the theatre had been spared.

"Wake up old man. We're stopping here for the night." Piet shook him. "Come on, you can share a room with me at the lodge. It'll be cheaper for us both. Their food is good and we'll have some red wine to go with it."

Avraham was impatient and had not expected to have to stop on the way. He sat next to Piet and watched him attack his food with gusto. In between mouthfuls he pointed a finger at Avraham's yarmulka. "You're a Jew aren't you?"

Avraham nodded. "What about you?"

"Me, I'm a Boer, but we both follow the Old Testament, so we're similar ya. I'll still teach you a little Afrikaans," and he laughed.

Their friendship was cemented with a glass of wine or two to the accompaniment of the men singing songs. Avraham couldn't understand the words but hummed along with them. Michael entertained them with card tricks until they retreated thankfully to bed.

Avraham felt unsteady on his feet. "Lovely wine," he mumbled holding onto Piet. He heard Piet saying something about gambling on the goldfields but his head felt fuzzy.

Piet helped him to bed and placed a blanket over him. "You remind me of my own Pa. He died when I was a little fellow."

Avraham felt a kinship with the younger man but the wine had taken effect, and closing his eyes, he was glad not to hear anymore of Piet's discourse on his card hands.

The wagon continued the next day and travelled a thousand miles to get to the goldfields with stops overnight along the way at various inns. The roads were bumpy and they traversed dangerous mountain passes. The mountain ranges had left Avraham feeling in awe of the beauty of his new country called the Cape of Good Hope. It had given him a sense of hope for the future and he was impatient to find gold.

Later that month, a letter arrived for Becky and Miriam. Miriam sat quietly at the table scrutinizing her mother's face.

"It seems your papa is enjoying himself. No thought for us working all the hours God made and more." Becky dropped the letter on the table and got up to make some supper.

Miriam raced through the letter. "It sounds so exciting," she said wishing she was rather with her father and read on:

Mt Nelson Boarding House
Room 24
Rand Goldfields,
Jan. 1887

My Dearest Becky and Miriam,

After a long,uneventful journey, I've at last arrived joining hundreds of other men hoping to get rich quick. The Afrikaners call us Uitlanders (Outsiders). We can't vote but that doesn't worry me. I'm here to make money. There are some corrupt officials. Thought I'd left this evil behind in the old country. Some men have started theatre productions and I went with Piet, a lovely young farmer, to see Hamlet. We have a good laugh watching McKay (he's from England) try and act. I met Piet on the passenger wagon and he's been like a son to me. He fell asleep and said he couldn't understand the actors – they weren't speaking proper English. I had to laugh at my Afrikaner friend. I think he sees me as a father figure and comes from a farm in the Elgin area, likes to gamble and insists I go along. Don't worry Becky, I haven't lost much money. There's not much to do here but the men know how to enjoy themselves. We watch a bit of boxing sometimes. Prospecting is a dusty job and I'm forever washing my clothes. Dust gets into everything. I wash in a tub outside. Piet makes growling noises but I know there are no wild animals around here. The only wild animals are people, all scrambling to find gold before the next man. There's plenty to eat here and we often cook meat outdoors when the sun goes down and it's not so hot. We have a shop here owned by a Mr Marks so I can buy everything I need.

You'll be pleased to hear that a congregation has been set up and I've been attending the Sabbath services. I miss you both and think of you every day. I know Monty and Esther will look after you whilst I'm away. Please write soon and tell me all your news.

Your beloved Avraham.

"Your papa misses me because he's never had to wash his own clothes, cook or clean in his life before. Fancies himself a gambling man does he? He hasn't lost much money yet, what next? And we haven't seen any of this money either. Naïve is what your papa is."

Becky shut the cupboard with a bang and Miriam winced. Becky stood red faced stirring the soup. "Soup's ready. There's a little meat in it. Miriam make yourself useful and get the bread."

"Mama, I'm not very hungry."

Becky dished up. "You eat this meat young lady. I'm not having you fade away. What suitors will fancy you then?"

Miriam was deep in thought. Joseph was never far from her thoughts and she wondered what he was doing. When would he write to her? How could she ever love another? She wasn't interested in suitors, how could any of them measure up to Joseph?

"Are you going to sit there forever dreaming?" Becky placed the soup on the table with a thud, sat down and ate in silence.

Miriam felt vexed. "You can't blame Papa for not sending us money yet. I'm sure he will do so soon. And besides, we're earning money thanks to Papa getting us a job in Monty's shop."

Becky looked up at Miriam who shivered seeing the cold look in her mother's eyes.

She woke during the night. Her dream was so strange where she'd called out to Joseph but had no answer. She shivered even though it was a hot summer's night and got up as quietly as she could to get some milk. Only there was none and she had a glass of water instead.

The next morning she woke with Becky shouting they would be late for work.

"A letter has arrived from Rachel. We'll read it later tonight. There's no time now, we mustn't be late," said Becky placing the letter on the table.

Miriam couldn't eat breakfast eager to know what Rachel had to say about Joseph. The day dragged and Dirk the farmer was back again.

Monty laughed. "You couldn't have gone through all that produce already. Must be feeding an army."

Dirk ignored the comment and approached Becky. "Would you and Miriam like to visit our farm?"

"We should like that very much," answered Becky with alacrity.

"Good, then I'll fetch you on Saturday morning at ten o'clock. You can sleep over at the farm. It's a long trek and I can't do it in one day."

Miriam looked at her mother and shook her head but her mother ignored her.

Monty thumped Dirk on the back. "Take as much time as you like. Becky and Miriam deserve a rest." He placed some money in Becky's hand. "Take this and think of it as a loan. Avraham can pay me back when I see him next."

Miriam had to listen to her mother talk of nothing else for the rest of the day. She could only think of Rachel's letter that was waiting for them. She was anxious to get home and irritated by her mother who was eager to see Dirk's farm in which she had no interest. At last it was time to go home and she had to listen to her mother deciding what they would wear for the visit.

"I think you should wear your blue dress. It shows off your blue eyes so well."

"Why are you so keen to visit Mr Uys' farm Mama?" asked Miriam reaching for the letter only to be stopped by a slap on the wrist.

"The letter's addressed to me. You'll have to wait until I've read it. Didn't Monty say Mr Uys is a successful farmer?"

Miriam felt vexed and wasn't the slightest bit interested whether Mr Uys was successful or not. She sat trying to tell by her mother's expression what news the letter could possibly contain.

Amersham Cottages,
No. 6
High Street
Amersham
London

My dearest Becky,

Since we saw you last so much has happened. Life is so different as I imagine yours must be too. Hannah's uncle offered Jacob a job in his factory where they make clothes and straw hats. I've watched how the women plait the straw and they work so hard. I'm so proud because Joseph has an important job as Factory Superintendent. We're living in a terraced house and share a garden with our neighbours. I've only said hello to them. I think they find my accent difficult to understand. I wish you were here to see the beautiful countryside. They use bricks to build houses here not wood like our homes in the Schtetl.

It's very cold here in winter and we light a fire to keep warm. The village has a horse drawn coach that goes to London town, but only Joseph has been and comes back with many stories to tell. I'm worried about Sarah. She's not been very well lately. I think the damp is no good for her. She hasn't been herself since we arrived in England and refuses to see a doctor. She's so stubborn. Jacob says that Joseph has landed in a pot of gold without having to prospect for it like Avraham. I like Hannah very much. I don't understand why Sarah finds fault with everything the poor girl does. We owe her so much. Jacob hasn't been himself either since we left home and hardly speaks at all these days. You remember how he and Sarah argued, well it's as if he doesn't hear Sarah anymore.

Becky, Hannah's family aren't religious. Her uncle, Mr Stern, persuaded Joseph to change our surname to Moffat. He says it'll be better for business and people will have trouble with the name Movsowitz. I try and talk to Jacob about it, but he says nothing as if he doesn't care anymore. If we had been in the old country, this would never have happened. I feel ashamed and Sarah just prays and thinks it's an ill-omen.

I have wonderful news to tell you. .Joseph and Hannah are getting married and Joseph said we'll be moving into a bigger house. He is taking good care of us all as I always knew he would. I spend my days looking after Sarah, washing, cooking and cleaning. Joseph says when he gets married, we'll have help in the house and I won't have to work so hard. I keep telling him it gives me something to do.

Has Avraham found gold yet? We hear lots of people are going to Africa to find gold. I keep thinking of when you lived next door and it took a few minutes to cross the path to your house. I miss you so much Becky and wish we were living in the same country. I think about you often and hope that you are all well. How is Miriam? She's constantly in Sarah's thoughts. Sarah constantly worries about Miriam. I'm sure she'll find a fine young man to marry.

Write soon Becky with all your news.

My love to you all,

Rachel

Becky handed the letter to Miriam. "It looks like they have an easier life than us."

Miriam felt her mother's eyes on her as she read the letter and bit her lip as she came to the part about Joseph and Hannah. Her vision blurred and she blinked. They sat in silence until Miriam, fingering the heart in her pocket, stood up.

"I'm tired Mama. I'm going to bed." She saw her mother's hand go to her mouth then wipe her eyes and didn't know whether she was upset about Rachel having an easier life or Joseph's forthcoming marriage and what that meant for her.

That night when she was sure her mother was asleep, her tears flowed for Joseph who she had to accept now would never be hers. She knew she'd been unrealistic to think it could have been any different. She remembered her mother once saying, "the match with Avraham was destined". Well, she was never sure about it being the hand of destiny. It had been after all an arranged marriage. If they'd still been in the Schtetl, they would have arranged a marriage between her and Joseph, and she was certain he would have grown to love her as her father loved her mother. Miriam swore that fate would not play a part in her life. She would decide her own destiny.

Saturday arrived soon enough. Miriam put on her blue dress and dabbed a little red lipstick on her lips. She glanced in the mirror in the hall while they waited. It was already hot at ten o'clock in the morning and at last Dirk arrived.

"Morning ladies," he said smiling broadly at Miriam. "Come Miriam, I'll help you and your ma onto the wagon." He took her hand and she didn't withdraw it.

Becky sat behind them holding a basket of food given to her by Esther for the journey. She opened a note that David had slipped in for Miriam. It said he had something important he wanted to ask her, and wanted to meet with her on her return. Becky was about to place it back in the basket when a sudden gust of wind caught the note, and it disappeared into the fir trees bordering the mountain pass.

The horses strained as they pulled the wagon over Sir Lowry's Pass. Dirk pointed out the Indian Ocean in the far distance. The deep blue of the sea and blue haze of the surrounding mountain ranges took Miriam's mind off Joseph and Hannah's impending marriage. She stared in awe.

Dirk smiled. "Wait till you see our farm."

She looked at Dirk, liked his rugged looks and handsome frame. He was tall with broad shoulders. Miriam reckoned it must come from working on the farm. She even liked his beard and he caught her looking at it.

"It's called a bokbaardjie. Do you like it?"

Miriam laughed. "What a funny name for a beard but yes, or ja as you say. I think it suits you." She caught her mother nodding and smiling to herself on the back seat of the wagon.

OUMA ROSIE'S FARM

"What do you farm?" asked Miriam, admiring the lush green Elgin Valley surrounded by a vast mountain range.

"We grow vegetables and have a herd of cattle."

She was aware of Dirk's eyes hovering over her, and began to think that life on a farm was undoubtedly better than living in a boarding house and working in Monty's dust-filled shop. The farmhouse loomed ahead. A large Dutch homestead with green shutters.

Miriam caught her breath. "It's beautiful." She saw a young black woman sweeping the verandah.

"Thembeki, would you go tell Ouma we've arrived. Come meet my Ouma," said Dirk, helping them off the wagon.

Ouma Rosie came into view wearing a black dress shrouding a formidable figure and greeted them with gusto. Miriam received a hug that almost left her breathless, whilst her mother's hand was grasped in a firm grip.

"Thembeki, don't just stand there and stare," shouted Ouma. "Go fetch some refreshments for our guests. Make sure you put out Cook's cake and fill the silver teapot with tea. Now be off with you." She led them inside the house and talked constantly without seeming to draw breath. "I insisted Dirk invited you, that way we can get to know each other a little." She gestured for them to sit down.

Miriam wondered why Ouma needed to get to know them? She was acutely aware of being given the once over by Ouma as she poured the tea. She talked non stop and all the while Miriam took in the rich velvet curtains and large fireplace. The room exuded an atmosphere of comfort and warmth that was very appealing.

"We have antelope, birds and leopards in the area. Did Dirk tell you?"

"Ouma, you talk too much. Give our guests a chance too." Dirk laughed.

"It's good to see you laugh for a change Dirk." Ouma turned to Miriam. "After tea, we'll go for a walk and show you around. I don't do much walking these days, my arthritis won't allow me. You must have a koeksister, they're sweet and just the thing to have with tea. Homemade you know."

Miriam noted an air of authority about this robust lady, and how Dirk did her bidding.

"These are delicious," said Becky licking her fingers and Miriam quickly passed her a serviette.

"Good, now we can take that walk," said Ouma addressing herself to Miriam and heaved herself up from the chair.

As they walked Miriam noticed a large group of black men and women picking vegetables and children running around playing. A few of the women had strapped babies onto their backs using blankets. "It must be hard to work in this heat," Miriam said walking fast to keep up with Ouma Rosie who didn't reply. She couldn't believe the old lady suffered from arthritis. Ouma headed for what looked like a large storeroom. It was cool inside and boxes were being filled with vegetables and carried out to a large ox-drawn wagon. Ouma sat down, wiping sweat from her brow.

Dirk introduced them to their Farm Manager. "We couldn't run this farm without Hendrik."

Hendrik greeted them and continued loading the wagon.

"You must leave early tomorrow. Get these vegetables to the market and stores, do you hear me Hendrik?" said Ouma with an air of authority.

"Ja Ouma, I'm trying but Thembo here is slow."

Miriam couldn't help notice how Hendrik's muscles gleamed with sweat in the hot African sun, as he lifted box after box with the help of Thembo, a young black boy. She was also aware of Hendrik's admiring glance.

Returning to the farm, Cook was preparing lunch and a wonderful aroma wafted towards them. Ouma stormed into the kitchen.

"What do you want Ouma?" asked Cook, a rotund figure and just as frightening to Miriam as Ouma Rosie. They had come in through the back door.

"Isn't lunch ready yet? What have you been doing? Must I stand behind you all the time?" Ouma's face was red and blotchy and the kitchen hot and sticky.

Steam rose from the stove and Miriam saw Cook's eyes glaze over. Dirk intervened and had he not she wasn't sure what might have happened.

"Looks like everything's in order to me," said Dirk taking Ouma by the hand and headed for the door followed by Miriam and Becky.

Ouma puffed out from the walk shouted, "Bring us the best red wine now," and swept past Cook who turned her back on Ouma.

They sat outside on the stoep whilst they waited for lunch. Thembeki brought them the wine and Ouma dozed off after a glass or two. Miriam and Dirk sat quietly in a corner with Miriam thankful for a respite from Ouma's incessant talking. The only sounds were flies buzzing around the dregs left in their wine glasses, and an orchestra of crickets chirping to their own music.

Becky got up quietly and followed the stoep around the side of the house. It overlooked the fields at the end of which were tall oak and poplar trees. In the far distance a mountain range rose up and encircled the valley. The wine had taken effect. She sat down and soon nodded off to sleep. She was woken by Miriam.

"Mama, lunch is ready," and Miriam whispered, "I'm sure I saw this farm in a dream. Isn't that strange?"

Becky shook her head. "I don't know what to make of you and your dreams. They're just dreams Miriam. I wouldn't put too much store by them. Don't know what your papa would make of all this." Murmuring under her breath, "But, like he said, we're not in the Schtetl anymore."

"You were the one who wanted to see Dirk's farm. Oh, never mind. We mustn't keep Ouma Rosie waiting."

"Yes, you can tell who the boss is around here," said Becky getting up slowly.

"Shh Mama. They're waiting for us."

Thembeki hovered around the lunch table, serving and making sure everyone was happy. Cook had gone off in a huff and they did not see her again that day. Thembeki prepared afternoon tea and later on a cold supper.

"I don't know what we'd do without Cook and Thembeki," remarked Dirk.

Miriam noticed Ouma either hadn't heard or maybe heard only when she wanted to.

In the evening Miriam and Dirk sat on the stoep. Miriam couldn't help see Ouma give Dirk a knowing smile as she said goodnight and went to bed. Becky took her cue and followed. Miriam relaxed and sipped a glass of wine. She felt a warm glow and found herself enjoying Dirk's company. She looked out onto the fields and could only imagine how it must feel to wake up to this green valley and mountains each day. She thought Dirk seemed more relaxed once his Ouma was not about, and discovered he had a sense of humour. They sat laughing and talking until late. When Dirk said goodnight his kiss was unexpected but she didn't resist.

When the time came to return to Cape Town. Eight oxen were being readied by Hendrik to pull the heavily laden wagon. Thembeki had made sure that Becky and Miriam were comfortable. She filled Miriam's basket with some of Cook's cold meat and home baked bread, taken from Cook's prized larder before she'd come into the kitchen that morning, and handed the basket to Miriam.

"Miss Miriam for you and your ma when you get hungry on the journey back to town."

"How thoughtful of you Thembeki. Please thank Cook and tell her we've enjoyed her delicious food and wonderful koeksisters."

Dirk followed them on his horse at a short distance, waving goodbye and shouted above the noise of the wind. "Miriam, I'll be coming to town next week again. Take good care of Miriam and her ma, Hendrik."

AVRAHAM'S RETURN JOURNEY

Returning home, there was a brief letter from Avraham.

"Your papa will be here on Friday night for supper with Esther and Monty." Becky looked up waving the letter in the air. She did a little dance. "He says he's found gold. We're going to be rich."

Miriam danced around the room with her mother until they heard banging coming from the next flat.

Friday morning dawned bright and sunny. When a customer walked into Monty's shop. Becky expected it to be Avraham. "When is he coming?"

"Be patient Becky." Monty pointed out, "it's a long journey."

That night they had supper as planned with Monty and Esther.

"Don't worry. He'll be here tomorrow, you'll see," said Monty reassuringly.

Miriam had a feeling something wasn't right.

The road was dusty and rough. The ox-wagon jolted from time to time as the oxen laboured in the heat of the day. They were pulled forward, up over the hills and down the other side. Before them always a mirage that teased and disappeared just as the wagon drew near. Avraham wiped his brow. The heat made him lethargic. The other half dozen men were dozing. The midday sun beat down relentlessly. He stretched out and was about to lie down when a muffled noise made him look back. He saw a cloud of dust. Horses seemed to rise up out of nowhere. He blinked, dazzled by the sun and sat up as the horses gathered speed, drawing nearer to their wagon. Instinctively, he felt for his money bag and shouted. "Jan, horses." The horses had drawn up alongside and then they were in front of the wagon. Jan whipped the oxen to go faster but it was too late. Shots rang out. Jan lashed out at a rider with his whip but was hit by a bullet. He fell backwards, hitting his head. Avraham felt the blood rush from his head and tried to retrieve his money bag from grasping hands. Saw a gun pointed at his head. He froze as a shot was fired and he lurched forwards.

Jan came to and looking down saw blood trickling from a wound on his arm. He turned around. Death stared back at him. Avraham's eyes were still open as he lay prostrate over another. Their guns lay unused by their sides. Jan got up shaking. It had happened so fast. In the silence that followed, he gently closed Avraham's eyes. Took blankets to cover the bodies and protect them from flies. Tore his shirt and tied it round his arm to stop the bleeding. Then took up the reins. He had to make it to Cape Town. Lifting his whip, the oxen slowly moved forward obeying his command. His head ached and he couldn't think straight. He didn't stop until he reached the city.

Miriam slept fitfully, waking to loud knocking. Half-awake she opened the door to two policemen. She couldn't absorb what they were saying. She felt faint. The story they told was gruesome. The wagon in which her father had been travelling had been intercepted by thieves. The men had been shot and killed with the exception of Jan van Jaarsveld. The thieves had made off with the loot, all the men's money made from prospecting.

The policeman said, "It had happened so fast, miss. They didn't have a chance. Van Jaarsveld brought your father's body back to town for burial."

Becky, who had been woken by voices, stood behind Miriam and let out an anguished cry. She buried her head in her hands. "What will I do without Avraham?"

Miriam was silent in her grief. She couldn't take it in.

"Mama, please ..." She hurried to put her arms around Becky who was clinging onto the curtains.

"Shall I call for a doctor, miss?" asked the policeman.

Becky looked blankly at him as Miriam guided her gently to a chair. "A doctor won't bring back my Avraham. What good is a doctor to me?" she wailed.

The policeman turned to Miriam. "Is there anyone I can call to help you and your mother?"

Esther sat with Becky all day. When Becky refused food, she insisted she had a little soup. Miriam was grateful for her presence.

She was at a loss to know what to do. Esther came each day with food and comfort. Without Esther, Miriam was sure her mother would have lost her mind. Her mother had always been in control. Now she wept and sat rocking in her chair all day.

Avraham was buried with the community rallying round. They arranged and paid for the funeral and the tea that followed in the synagogue hall. The Rabbi's last words echoed in Miriam's ears, "There is no death," he said quietly, looking in the direction of Miriam. She was too grief stricken for his words to have any impact.

She was grateful to Dirk, who came as soon as he heard of the tragedy and conveyed Ouma Rosie's condolences.

Jan van Jaarsveld approached Miriam after the funeral. "It'll never happen again. Next time I'll be ready for the swines."

It was no consolation for Miriam or her mother. She could barely absorb what he said. Her shock turned to anger. Her father had made them leave a country where he said violence lurked in the shadows. This country was no different now in her eyes. In the following weeks she struggled to look after her mother as best she could. Esther visited often and took Becky out but her mother seemed lifeless. She was losing weight and had begun to take on a frail appearance. It took all of Miriam's strength to get through each day in Monty's shop. Her mother was no longer up to working in the shop. It was now up to her to change their fortune. Dirk came to town more often and stayed overnight with Monty and Esther. She looked forward to seeing him at the shop and having supper with him at Esther and Monty's home. It was a reprieve from a grief stricken mother although she felt guilty leaving her mother at home. Dirk's presence was a comfort and she wondered about his intentions. She was lonely and missed his company when he had to return to the farm.

Weeks went by before Dirk came to town again. When he arrived at the store she was happy to see him and went to greet him.

Dirk led her into the office. "Good day Monty. Would you mind if I used your office for a short while? I need to speak to Miriam."

"Of course not, but don't be too long you two," said Monty walking out with a grin on his face.

Miriam looked at Dirk with a puzzled look. "Is something wrong Dirk? Is it Ouma?"

He shook his head. "There's something I want to ask you Miriam." Shifting from foot to foot he took a deep breath. "Will you marry me?"

Miriam felt her heart beating fast. She hesitated and words tumbled out. "I have no dowry to offer you Dirk, and you know I'm Jewish."

"Miriam, a number of your people have intermarried with us Boers, and you'll be accepted by our community. I love you Miriam. I'll be good to you."

Miriam was thinking of Joseph. Nothing would have stood in her way of marrying Joseph had he asked her. "I don't know what my mama would say?"

"We'll work that one out. I want you, not your dowry. Miriam, you haven't given me an answer yet."

Miriam made a decision. "I'll marry you Dirk, but please could we keep it to ourselves until I've had a chance to tell my mama. Let me speak to her before you fetch us for supper tonight."

Miriam blushed every time Dirk looked at her in the shop. It was difficult to concentrate and while she sorted the shelves her mind was buzzing.

Dirk needed a wife and she needed security. He need never know that a part of her heart would always belong to Joseph. After all, arranged marriages back home in the Shtetl lasted a lifetime. And this suited both of them. She enjoyed his company and he was a good man. She was sure her papa had liked him. There was no time to worry what people might think of her marrying out of the faith. She would have to think about a wedding dress and an outfit for her mama.

Arriving home Miriam led her mama to the kitchen. "I have some news Mama. Dirk has asked me to marry him."

Becky sat down slowly.

"Mama, did you hear me?"

"Oh, I heard you alright. Have you forgotten you're Jewish? Whatever would your papa say?"

"Mama, I have no dowry and as for Papa, he liked Dirk and would have been happy for me. Dirk told me a number of Jews have intermarried in his community. I've spared you from knowing that Jewish teachers and children are excluded from state-subsidized schools. And, I've been told they're debarred from military posts, positions of president, state secretary or magistrates and membership in parliament."

Becky covered her face with her hands. "That's enough. I don't want to hear anymore."

"Mama, you need to know that Jews are considered foreigners and excluded from mainstream life in South Africa."

"So much for your papa saying we would be safe in this country. I'm against intermarriage whatever Dirk says."

Miriam knew she had to tell her Mama but didn't know how and finally blurted it out, "Mama, I'll need to convert to marry Dirk." Miriam took a step back seeing her mama's thunderous look. Becky hauled herself up and was about to walk out of the kitchen.

"Please listen to me Mama. My mind is made up. You'll like Dirk once you get to know him. You loved the farm and you'll love living in such a beautiful part of the country." Miriam felt her knees go and she grabbed the arm of the chair. This was an enormous decision and needed her mama's blessing.

Becky turned round, "You're forsaking your religion," and pointed a finger at Miriam, "I'm not going to live on the farm with that old woman."

"That old woman is Dirk's grandma and she is a kind and god-fearing lady."

Becky shook her head slowly. "You think the Afrikaner community will accept you? You think you know his grandma do you? Well, I tell you she's a hard woman and won't be easy to live with.

I'm staying right here."

Miriam sighed. "Mama, you can't stay here on your own and you know that. Dirk is coming to fetch us for supper. Please think about my happiness and give Dirk a chance."

"I'm staying home. Food will stick in my throat," and Becky sat down putting her head in her hands.

"Mama, this place is not home. I have a chance to make life better for both of us. Please don't cry Mama."

"If we'd stayed in the Shtetl your papa would still be alive, and this would never have happened. I could have arranged a good marriage for you."

Miriam swallowed. "Mama, that's in the past. I have to think of what's best for me right now."

There was a knock on the door. Becky got up and went to her room slamming the door behind her, leaving Miriam staring after her. Opening the front door she burst into tears when she saw Dirk. "It's Mama, we don't have her blessing Dirk."

He put his arm around Miriam. "Your mama will come round. Give her time."

Supper that evening at Monty and Esther was a sombre affair.

Esther took her aside the next morning at work. "My dear Miriam, I am so sorry but it's too far for us to travel to the farm for your wedding, and I've not been too well lately."

"I understand Esther. I hope it's nothing serious?" but she had a feeling Esther didn't want to attend the wedding because it was to be held in a church.

Ouma liked Miriam and it didn't matter to her that Miriam was Jewish. She'd given up believing in God after her prayers went unanswered and she lost her beloved husband, Jannie. No matter how many times Dominee begged her to attend his church she stood her ground.

"Dominee's coming to lunch today, Cook. I want you to make

his favourite dish – roast lamb."

When Ouma Rosie was out of earshot, Cook turned to Thembeki, "Wonder what Ouma's up to. Must want something from him."

Thembeki shrugged her shoulders and set to laying the table. "Why haven't Miriam and Becky been invited for lunch today?"

"How must I know? I'm the cook and can't see inside that head of Ouma's."

Dirk went to fetch Dominee, and Rusty's barks alerted them to their arrival at the farm.

"Thembeki, go get our finest wine from the cellar and look after Dominee you hear," said Ouma fussing over the table setting. Every time Dominee's wine glass was empty Ouma Rosie nodded in Thembeki's direction and she quickly filled it.

Thembeki watched in amazement as Dominee kicked Rusty.

Disappearing into the kitchen Thembeki said, "Something's wrong. Dominee is kicking Rusty and Ouma says nothing."

"Good. I hate that dog and Dominee," said Cook, wiping her hands on her apron. "The dog steals my food, and Dominee drinks all our wine. You'd think a Reverend would know better."

Thembeki returned to the dining room where Rusty's head was on the table waiting for scraps. The Dominee pushed him away roughly and Rusty yelped. Ouma remained silent. Eventually they retired to the stoep with wine glasses in hand. Dominee held on to the furniture as he made his way outdoors.

Ouma said, "Dominee, do you remember how we helped you fix the church roof?"

"Ja, very grateful," he replied and reached for more wine.

"Ja, well now I need your help and blessing, Dominee."

Dirk watched Dominee trying to keep awake.

"I want you to convert Miriam," and paused, "and marry my Dirk and Miriam."

"What?" he opened one eye. "Ouma, you told me Miriam's Jewish. I can't marry them in my church."

"You didn't hear me Dominee. I want you to convert Miriam. Have you forgotten that Jesus was Jewish. The Jews are 'People of the Bible,' and we both follow the Old Testament. You told me yourself," said Ouma with a smile.

Dirk watched Dominee open both eyes. He knew Dominee would be fighting a losing battle against Ouma.

Ouma filled Dominee's glass herself. "What else needs fixing in your church? Dirk and I will be very happy to help you."

Dominee gave Ouma a quizzical look. "You know I have a list of things that need fixing in the church."

"Exactly Dominee. Let's shake hands. You convert her and marry my Dirk and Miriam, and I will help you tackle that list of yours." Ouma grabbed his hand and shook it vigorously. The wine had taken its toll, with his hand still in Ouma's firm grip, his head dropped forward onto his chest. Ouma released her hand from his grip and smiled at Dirk as Dominee snored softly.

RACHEL'S LETTER, 1888

Amersham Cottages	Kaya Lami Farm,
No. 6	Elgin Valley
High Street	The Cape
Amersham	South Africa
England	11th November, 1888

Dear Becky,

I would not want to begin a letter with sad news but Sarah passed away a little over a month ago. She was always so full of life. It was sad to see her go downhill so quickly. She kept saying how much she missed Miriam – if only she could see her one more time. My heart ached for her. I feel her loss terribly as we were so close.

I'm so sorry for not writing sooner but my time was taken up looking after Sarah. Now, I must try and find things to fill the time, not like before in the Schtetl. Do you remember how hard we worked from morning till night? So much to do but we always made time for a cup of Russian tea together. Now it's English tea that we drink with milk. I can't get used to it.

Hannah is very kind but I don't feel this is home. I'm always checking with Hannah if it's alright to do this or that, you know what I mean. I'm not complaining of course. We're so fortunate to have such a good son and daughter-in-law.

I do have some good news to tell you, Hannah is pregnant and I'm so looking forward to being a bobba. I hope I'll be able to help Hannah because I've not been very well lately. I've lost weight and feel tired all the time. Hannah insists on getting a housekeeper so I don't work too hard and Joseph is taking me to see the doctor.

Jacob hasn't changed. Still doesn't say much, just sits with his head in the newspaper. Joseph taught him to read a little. He doesn't listen to me when I talk to him or maybe it's his hearing. I like to talk to Hannah and she lets me help her a little in the kitchen.

The factory is doing well and Joseph says that they've had to employ more women in the sewing department where they make dresses and straw hats. They have a shop front where a few items are displayed. We'll need more space when the baby arrives, so Joseph and Hannah are planning to buy a bigger house.

Joseph takes me for lovely walks. He thinks all I need is fresh air. There are a few dairy farms in the area. You would love our village Becky. We have quite a few shops – butcher; baker; grocer and stationer. I'm getting forgetful. I might have told you all this before? There's also a pub where Hannah's uncle takes Joseph and Jacob for a drink. Jacob doesn't like the pub much but he doesn't want to cause offence and must be grateful for having a job. I'm not sure what Jacob does at the factory and he doesn't talk about it. But then, he never was much of a talker, was he Becky?

I wish you could visit. You'll be pleased to hear there's a synagogue in the village which I confess I haven't been to yet.

Jacob doesn't seem to want to go anywhere so Joseph takes me out when he can. We've walked past the local school called Back Lane School. I've peeked inside where there are long desks where the children sit and seen them use slates and slate pencils. Joseph told me they sharpen their pencils on the school walls outside. What a funny thing to do. Hannah has taken me to the weekly market where we buy our vegetables, and there's an annual fair that Joseph promises to take me to next. He says they sell perfume, exotic fruit called oranges and fine wood carvings. You can even buy furs, if you can afford such a luxury from merchants who travel throughout England. Even so, I miss our life in the Schtetl and all of you.

Write to me soon Becky. I want to hear all your news and please God this letter finds you all in good health.

Your loving friend always,
Rachel

THE WEDDING

Miriam stood in front of the mirror listening with half an ear to her mother. Dirk's proposal after the death of her father made her feel she could breathe again. Leaving every morning for work and asking Esther to look in on her mother had weighed her down. Mother and daughter roles had reversed and she was feeling resentful.

How had so much happened in such a short space of time? In the Schtetl there would have been a period of time required for a courtship. She felt like a ship without a rudder in Africa with her mother still grieving for her father.

"Do you love Dirk? Miriam, did you hear me?"

"Sorry Mama, what did you say?" She couldn't get the thought of Hannah having Joseph's baby out of her head. To hear this news before her wedding had thrown her. After all that had happened she still felt the pain of Joseph's rejection.

Was she never going to be able to forget?

"Do you love Dirk? I worry you haven't known each other for that long."

Miriam bit her lip. "You're asking me now? Isn't it a bit late? Sorry Mama."

She hugged her mother. "Dirk is a good man, Mama. I respect him and you've even grown fond of him. In a way it's like an arranged marriage. Only I've done the arranging."

Becky raised her eyebrows and carried on clipping the veil to Miriam's hair. "Yes, he is a good man," and under her breath muttered, "can't say the same for his Ouma."

She moved to the window. "It's time to go. The carriage has arrived."

Miriam laughed. "You mean cart." She hurried over and looked out of the window. "It's beautiful Mama. Bedecked with flowers and even the horse is decorated with flowers."

"Hurry Miriam. We don't want to be late for the ..." Becky couldn't say the word church.

Miriam took her mother's hand, "Mama, I promise I won't forget my roots."

Becky merely nodded and said, "It's done now."

She hadn't told her mama that Dominee had kindly arranged for a colleague to convert her in Cape Town. Nor the fact that Jews who converted were known as Boer Jews. She didn't want to cause any more heartbreak for her mama.

Ouma Rosie called from downstairs, "Miriam, we mustn't keep Dominee waiting."

"Is that all she's worried about?" muttered Becky.

"Shh, Mama. Help me down the stairs. I'm scared I'll trip over this long veil."

Miriam stood admiring Dominee's church overflowing with pink proteas and lily of the valley. The scent filtered to where she waited to walk down the aisle. She was sure her papa would have been happy for her. But she had misgivings about her mama living under the same roof as Ouma. She'd tried to reassure her mama by referring to Ouma as tough as the dried meat they called biltong but having a tender heart. It was a relief when her mama finally agreed to live on the farm.

She was glad that Hendrik had agreed to walk her down the aisle. When at last the organist began to play, Hendrik took her arm and they began to walk slowly down the aisle. She loved the flowers adorning her long curly hair and the lace wedding dress nipped in at the waist. It showed off her voluptuous figure. She felt a little dizzy, partly because she hadn't eaten breakfast and she couldn't still the worry in her mind. Converting and marrying in a church made her fear she might be punished for forsaking Judaism. But hadn't her papa said the Afrikaner also followed the Old Testament. She saw Dirk's look of admiration and it made her bury any misgivings. An image of Joseph made her close her eyes briefly before continuing down the aisle towards Dirk.

She admired Dirk who looked handsome in a suit with a fob watch that Ouma had given him. His beard reminded her of Joseph as they stood before Dominee. She was a little unsteady on her feet and she smiled to herself as a thought occurred to her. What other young woman would've been happy to share a home with Ouma? Passing the pews packed with guests she noticed the farm labourers sitting at the back. She'd been warned by Dirk who expected members of the congregation to come out of curiosity to see her. He told her that rumours had spread he was marrying a Jewish girl and Dominee was welcoming her to his flock.

Ouma turned to see Becky wiping her eyes as Dominee pronounced them man and wife. "For goodness' sake, it's a day for celebration not tears Becky. Don't let Miriam see you crying." Ouma handed Becky a handkerchief.

Church bells began to ring as Miriam stepped outside into the glare of the African sun with Dirk. Becky kissed her and walked slowly behind Ouma as they approached the cart to take them back to the farm house for the celebrations.

♣ ♣ ♣

On the farm, Hendrik was already busy roasting a lamb over the spit with the help of Thembo. Coals were smouldering much like Cook in the kitchen.

"So much to do. Where's the help Ouma promised?" fumed Cook.

Thembeki was looking out of the kitchen window. "They're coming. I can see them walking up the path now," she shouted and ran outside to show the African women the way to the kitchen. Six young women entered the kitchen and stared at Cook. She threw them aprons and locked eyes with them like an angry bull. They stood rooted to the spot.

"Well, get to work. Don't just stand there. There's plenty needs doing," said Cook up to her eyes in steam standing over a hot stove. She pointed to the bowls of assorted salads. "They must all be put on the trestle tables outside, and when you're done I'll show you how to cut the watermelons." Dozens of watermelons lay on the floor. "Do you have names?" Cook asked.

One of the African women coughed and said. "I'm Winnie, this is Grace and …"

Cook interrupted. "Alright, alright, I don't have time to remember all your names. Put those aprons on and get to work."

Thembeki plied the girls with tea and biscuits and then heard Ouma call her. She hurried out with one last look at the sweat on the foreheads of the young girls as they laboured under Cook's watchful eye.

Guests sat under umbrellas at tables and chairs that had been arranged in the garden. Thembeki rushed up to Miriam.

"Miss Miriam, you look like a princess."

Miriam laughed and gave Thembeki a hug.

Ouma pointed to a tray of tall wine glasses filled to the brim. "Hurry Thembeki. See all our guests have wine and make sure Dominee is topped up and happy."

Miriam was fond of Thembeki, who had told her she knew all the farmers and some of their secrets. She smiled to herself remembering their conversation.

"Miss Miriam, all the farm workers gather once a week on Sundays and trade stories about their Masters and Madams. I just laugh but my ma and pa taught me to be loyal to the people you work for, and I'm very fond of Ouma and Dirk and even Cook."

Miriam couldn't help but laugh herself. "Cook is quite formidable, isn't she Thembeki?"

"Formidabal? What does that mean Miss Miriam?"

Miriam had screwed up her face and Thembeki laughed. "She can be quite forceful like Ouma, but don't tell her."

"No Miss Miriam. I'm like a lamb with both of them."

Miriam knew she could rely on Thembeki and looking around Thembeki was a friendly face in a crowd of people she didn't know.

The tables were laden with a variety of salads and meat from the braai. This was followed by watermelon. Cook gave the young African girls coffee and Cape brandy tarts for each table.

"Don't just stand there, take these brandy tarts and start serving before I bring this frying pan down on your heads."

"A wonderful feast, Ouma," said Dominee, raising his glass.

Ouma slipped a packet into his coat pocket "Now don't stop at the 'Watering Hole' on your way home, you hear, ja?"

Miriam mingled with the guests. It was as she passed one table she heard farmers talking about the possibility of war with the English. She felt a knot in her stomach with the ugly smell of war about.

One of the farmer's wives handed Miriam a present. "We know you'll be living in the old farm house with Ouma Rosie, but this gift is for when you make your own home."

Miriam was quick to reply. "Thank you, but this is my home," and returned to Dirk's side wondering how she was going to remember the names of everyone he introduced her to. Eventually, wandering over to her mother who looked lost amidst the crowd of people, Miriam sat down and took her hand. "Mama you look worried. You'll find Dirk's an easy man to get along with."

"If you say so, but it's not him I'm worried about." Becky pointed to Ouma who was talking to Dominee.

Miriam checked Ouma wasn't looking their way before replying, "I know how to handle Ouma."

"You might be able to but can I?"

Miriam watched the guests dancing to boere music. Dirk was busy talking and she decided to see what was happening in the barn that had been cleared for the farm workers. Walking arm in arm with her mother, they stood at the entrance.

There was plenty of food and drink and a trestle-table groaned with food and wine.

Miriam whispered to her mother. "This looks like more fun."

"We shouldn't be here. We should go back now," but Becky didn't move, watching open mouthed.

Miriam watched one of the men take out his mouth organ, another a piano accordion and yet another a yukeleli. The dancing got started to the sounds of robust singing and stamping. Miriam watched Cook grab a man, hitch up her skirt and lose herself in a liberated dance.

"See those tree trunks," said Koos, one of the farm hands, pointing to Cook's legs, "her man couldn't have seen those before they walked up the aisle," and put his head back, roaring like a lion.

Becky laughed out loud.

"Shh Mama, you'll give us away," said Miriam peering round the barn door.

"Ja, but she can bake better than your wife," grinned another man, showing two front teeth missing.

Miriam looked at her mother and this time they both burst out laughing. Miriam could see sweat pouring off Cook. She spotted Thembeki letting her hair down and was glad they were also enjoying themselves. She gave her mother a tug and they walked back to the wedding party slowly, still laughing.

At the end of the evening and the guests all gone, Miriam stood watching the sun set. The mountains were bathed in a misty blue with a sky painted a pale pink hue. She made her way indoors after Dirk said he'd be up soon. Ouma Rosie and her mama had retired to bed. Miriam made her way upstairs aware of how silent the countryside was at night.

She changed out of her wedding dress and waited for Dirk with trepidation, wondering why he was taking such a time. Then she heard his footsteps. He walked in with a bottle of wine and glasses. She relaxed after two glasses of wine, and lying in bed Dirk kissed her gently. She felt his hand under her nightie caressing her breasts. His touch made her skin tingle and ignited a desire she'd never felt before. He began to stroke her seeking the most intimate part of her body. The wine had taken effect. She closed her eyes. Aroused she arched her back as he entered her responding to his thrusts until they both fell back onto the pillows exhausted. Whispering he loved her he was asleep within minutes. Miriam listened to his breathing as they lay in each other's arms, but she couldn't sleep. Her mind wandered to how it might have felt had it been Joseph making love to her. She had brought the wooden heart with her and hid it rather like Joseph hidden within her mind. She couldn't stop his image emerging even when Dirk was making love to her. Eventually she fell asleep feeling the warmth of Dirk's body beside her.

Dominee had enough of playing the straight-laced church man. He left as the dancing started and headed for his favourite watering hole.

"Hullo Dominee," said Jan, looking up from wiping glasses at the bar. "What are you doing here? Had enough of the wedding?"

"Had enough. No one to dance with. Can't watch the old aunties dance. They'd have my head off if I asked one of their daughters to dance."

"Didn't know you were scared of the old aunties Dominee," laughed Jan, handing him a glass of wine.

"No, of course not, but I have to fill my church pews otherwise I'll be sent to some dorp in the desert. Why don't you join me in a little drink? Ah, there's Christiaan, come man and join your Dominee." Dominee pointed a finger up to heaven. "You know the British want to annex our Boer republics and overthrow our Boer government. That man they call 'Sir' Alfred Milner, the Cape Colony governor. Ja, and then there's the 'gold bugs' and 'outsiders.' Miriam's father was an 'outsider' prospecting on the gold mines."

"What do you mean 'gold bugs'?" Jan looked at him puzzled.

"Dominee means the owners of the gold mines man," answered Christiaan.

"President Kruger won't allow them to do that, you'll see," answered Jan confidently.

Dominee was soon nodding off.

Jan beckoned to Christiaan. "Take the old man home. He can't hold his liquor and he's had enough for one day."

When Dominee woke up the next morning, the packet given to him by Ouma was open on his bedside table. He remembered stopping off at the bar on his way home. Sharing a drink with Jan and the others was one of the few pleasures he had in this life. There was no wife to warm his bed. No women in the town wanted to be his wife so he gave up trying. He was grateful to Ouma Rosie for supporting his church. She had been good to him, welcoming him into her home. He was sure he could count on Ouma's financial support when she needed another blessing for the family.

BECKY'S LETTER, 1890

Kaya Lami Farm
Elgin Valley
The Cape
South Africa

Amersham Cottages
No. 6 High Street
Amersham
England
7th November, 1890

Dear Rachel,

I am sorry for not writing sooner but when you read my letter I hope you'll understand. It was wonderful receiving your letter with all your news. It took me back to the times we used to sit over a cup of tea and talk. I am so sad to hear about Sarah's death. I wish you all a long life. Miriam hardly ever talks about the past. Maybe that's for the best. For me, I live in the past. There doesn't seem to be a place for me here now that Avraham's gone. He was killed by thieves who attacked their wagon coming back from the gold fields. It was a terrible time for me and life is empty without him. Miriam is now my strength. Without her and the help from friends, Monty and Esther Herman, I would have lost the will to live. Avraham thought he was bringing us to a safe country. I don't believe such a place exists. But there, I'm beginning to sound like a bitter old woman.

My news is that Miriam has married an Afrikaner farmer, Dirk Uys. We are living on a farm with his Ouma as he calls her, or grandmother in the Elgin Valley. I wish you could see it. It's so beautiful with mountains surrounding the whole valley. There's a river nearby where you can swim and have picnics. My joy would be complete if only Avraham was here. Dirk isn't Jewish but he's a good man and I've grown fond of him. Monty and Esther live in Cape Town so we hardly ever see them now, as it's a long journey to Elgin. Sometimes

Miriam and I go with Dirk to Cape Town for supplies but the journey is long and tiring by ox-wagon. Life on a farm is very different and I don't like to complain but I do get very lonely. Ouma is a hard woman but I get on well with her cook. She's an African woman who was born on this farm. To pass the time I knit and sew a little.

I hope we'll hear more often from you. How strange that we've both ended up living with our children. Avraham always swore that he would never do so but I haven't any choice and I suppose you don't either. Rachel, I miss you and our old lives. We were such a close community. There's a small Jewish community here, but I'm in an awkward position as Miriam is now part of the Afrikaner community. I don't want to make life difficult for her. Ouma runs this farm with Hendrik who seems to have a hand in everything. Dirk is away a lot of the time going to political meetings. I know nothing about the politics in this country. Dirk talks about a bad feeling between the Afrikaner and the British. He thinks they might go to war against the British. There's no safe country in the world for anyone is there? Can you believe it, I talk to Dominee, he's the Reverend of the local church. He's always here for lunch on Sundays, and he's a good man, although I don't know what Avraham would have made of his drinking habit.

You must write soon, and tell me about your life in England and all about the baby. Give my love to the family.

Your loving friend always,

Becky

~ ~ ~

Ouma marched into the room where Miriam was busy sewing and declared, "It's enough of sitting and sewing. Time for you to learn something about farming."

Miriam stared at Ouma. Now what had she done wrong?

"Don't look at me like that. A woman who doesn't bear children must make herself useful in other ways. Come with me."

It was an order and no use arguing, as Miriam knew too well. She put her sewing aside. Ouma she'd learnt was strong willed and when an idea was embedded in her mind, nothing and no one would change it. She got up and followed Ouma but her comments were hurtful. It was hard enough not falling pregnant without Ouma making it feel like a punishment. Her mother kept telling her to relax and it would happen. What chance did she have when Dirk spent so much time away from her attending political meetings. When he did return he and Dominee would talk long into the night until the wine took effect and conversation died. The smooth running of the farm was thanks to Hendrik.

Ouma headed for Hendrik's office above the large store and shouted. "Hendrik, I want you to teach Miriam how to keep the books."

"Ouma, I know nothing about book-keeping." Miriam looked at Hendrik for support.

"Don't worry, Miriam. I'll teach you and it's not as hard as you think. Come and sit down." Hendrik drew a chair up for her and made tea for them both.

Miriam heard Ouma shouting at Thembeki and squirmed in the chair.

"What are you doing following us around? You're like Miriam's shadow. I'm not going to harm the girl. She must earn her keep like us all. Now get back to your duties."

One Sunday after lunch, Dirk and Dominee had too much to drink and Dirk raised his glass exclaiming, "In 1881 at the mountain of Majula, the Boers beat the British," and slapped his thigh. "That was the day David toppled Goliath," to which both men raised their glasses.

"Why were you fighting the British?" asked Miriam with half an eye on wine spilt on her newly embroidered tablecloth. "War is an anathema."

"Maybe so," mumbled Dominee, "but the British taxed our farmers, annexed the Transvaal, controlled our native districts and our foreign affairs. In 1884, at the Convention of London, control was handed back to us Boers. The British took a beating militarily and politically – a just desert." Having run out of breath he downed the rest of his wine.

"Their pride has been wounded – the dogs," sneered Dirk.

Miriam sensed their hatred and felt a darkness close in on her. She listened as talk continued about the possibility of another war with the British.

Ouma turned to Dirk. "You need to attend to farm matters once in a while."

Dirk brought his hand down hard on the table. "There are more important things to concern ourselves with now, Ouma."

"Oh yes, and what's that exactly?" Ouma's voice reached a high pitch.

"There's talk about another war with the British," said Becky.

Ouma turned on Becky. "Do you think I don't know. Do you take me for an imbecile?"

"Of course not," replied Becky turning to Miriam for support.

Miriam saw her mama's wounded look and knew life wasn't easy for her mother living in the same house as Ouma. She thought of the first time she and her mama had gone to look at Cook's kitchen. She recalled the conversation that transpired. Cook made them tea and said nothing when they had sat down at her kitchen table. Miriam hadn't realised how lonely her mama was until then. When they were in Cook's kitchen, her mama spoke for the first time. Her mama had said, "There's nothing for me to do in this house."

Miriam had held her mama's hand all the while she talked about home in the Schtetl with Avraham.

"Miss Becky, you could show me your Jewish recipes," said Cook.

Miriam remembered her mama's shaky voice. "But what will Ouma say?"

Cook answered, "Ag, she won't even know it's Jewish food," and had winked at Thembeki. "Thembeki will tell her you're showing me new recipes."

Thembeki had raised her voice. "Why don't you tell Ouma? You're the Cook not me."

Miriam felt relief that her mama got on with Cook. She'd been lost in thought until she heard the word 'England' that brought her back to the present.

"Did you say something about England?" asked Becky.

"Why don't you listen, are you deaf?" Ouma said.

Miriam could hear Ouma's voice rising in pitch.

"Farmers are getting into fruit farming and all you're interested in is politics. Don't you remember the article in the newspaper?" Ouma turned on Dirk. When he didn't reply she continued, "Our neighbours have long been producing fruit and exporting to England. We're going back to 1892 when fruit was sent in the *Drummond Castle* ship. I don't remember how much their fruit was sold for, but farmers in our area are growing pears, grapes, nectarines and even apples. And what are we still growing – potatoes, onions, pumpkins, beans and tomatoes."

Dirk topped up his glass. "When our neighbours are successful I'll think about going into farming fruit. I know all about the refrigeration chamber that was tried out in the *Grantully Castle*. That experiment was a failure. Food was rotten by the time it reached England."

"I don't see why it can't be done." Ouma's voice reached a crescendo. "The Tasmanians have been shipping apples and pears to England since 1891. Didn't you read about peaches being sent on the *Drummond Castle* ship? They sold for 2s.3d. each in Covent Garden. Maybe you were at one of your important meetings?"

Dirk shifted in his chair. "Some of us have to concern ourselves about the future of this country."

"If you're not interested why not ask Hendrik to find out about fruit farming?"

Dirk replied in a quietly controlled voice. "I didn't say I wasn't interested. We don't have the money to invest in planting any fruit orchards."

"Borrow from the bank then," snapped Ouma.

"You know very well the bank won't loan us any more money."

"When all the other farmers get rich then don't complain." Ouma moved the bottle of wine out of Dirk's reach.

"We'll wait and see if they get rich shall we?" Dirk got up.

Ouma shouted, "You know what's been said that there are great possibilities for the apple trade. Ag, you won't listen to an old woman. You're stubborn as an ox just like your father." Ouma squinted in the sun, turning to Miriam. "Other farmers believe fruit will travel well if they are packed properly and refrigeration is correctly controlled."

Miriam looked from Ouma to Dirk, who stood up towering over Ouma, his legs straddled and arms folded across his chest.

"When they've solved the refrigeration problem I'll consider planting fruit," said Dirk.

"You would do well to remember one thing Dirk," said Ouma. "We're all in this business together." With that Ouma took herself off without another backward glance.

That evening Dirk led Miriam upstairs to their bedroom. His sexual attentions were few and far between. She had a feeling that it was either the wine or anger behind his need for her. She felt a sense of loneliness because all he talked about were his meetings with other Afrikaners and their grievances against the British. She thought of Joseph and how they used to share their thoughts and feelings. She didn't have that with Dirk. Listening to Dirk snore and unable to sleep, she listened to the sounds of Africa. Crickets chirping outside the open window.

When she woke the next morning there was a dent in the bed where Dirk had lain. She got up to close the window and thought about Ouma's words. Looking across the fields, she spotted an old gnarled apple tree surrounded by vegetables. Maybe Ouma was right and they should be following the example of other farmers and planting an apple orchard.

♣ ♣ ♣

Miriam touched her stomach gently and looked at herself in the mirror. She hadn't eaten anything that could have made her feel this nauseas. She'd wait another month. Keep this wondrous news to herself a little longer. But it was a battle not to think what it would have felt like had it been Joseph's child. Two months later when she was sure she drew Dirk aside and now the excitement took over as she said, "We're going to have a baby."

"You're pregnant," he shouted lifting her up and putting her down gently. "Come on, let's tell Ouma." Taking her by the hand they announced their happy news. Cook and Thembeki came running to see what all the commotion was about. Thembeki clapped her hands and Cook beamed with delight.

"Don't cry Mama," said Miriam hugging her mother.

"Oh Miss Miriam, it'll be wonderful to fill this farmhouse with children." Thembeki hugged Miriam spontaneously.

"Hang on a minute Thembeki, one baby at a time," said Dirk as he filled their glasses with wine. "Here's to another Uys."

"Another Uys at long last," said Ouma but a smile lit up her face as she reached for a glass of wine.

Miriam felt relieved that Dirk's preoccupation with the business of war was, for the moment, far from his thoughts.

1899, THE 2ND ANGLO-BOER WAR

Miriam breastfed baby Tania with a blanket strategically placed, whilst sitting away from the others. It was a hot day and she was glad of the homemade lemonade that Thembeki brought. She tried not to smile when she caught sight of Dominee looking at the jug in disgust while politely accepting a glass.

"Miriam must have lots to drink when breastfeeding," said Ouma.

Miriam felt Dirk's hand on her shoulder and wondered at his hesitation when he said. "Umm … we're grouping at Magersfontein. I may be away for some time. Now don't worry Ouma, I've spoken to Hendrik and he'll look after the farm."

Ouma leaned forward in her rocking chair almost tilting it over. "You're going to war?"

Dirk put his hand out to steady the rocker, and Miriam saw a look of horror on Ouma's face that reflected exactly how she felt when Dirk first told her.

"You knew what my meetings were about, so why are you looking so surprised Ouma?"

"I didn't think the talking would end in war," said Ouma, leaning right back.

Dominee put his hand out to steady Ouma's rocker. "War with the British is inevitable. I'll look after your family while you're gone Dirk, don't worry. They won't touch a Dominee."

The men spoke quietly and Miriam leaned forward to catch every word.

Dirk's voice was solemn. "We've been given two rifles each by Kruger. The British have troops between the Cape and Natal, and Kruger has given them an ultimatum to withdraw. They say that Commander White's force has been trapped in Natal and we're besieging them in Mafeking and Kimberley. They won't negotiate, so it's war Ouma."

Miriam handed the baby to Thembeki, who strapped Tania on to her back with the blanket. "We'll manage on the farm and Dirk will be back soon," she said and could see Ouma was distraught. She felt more worried about Ouma than herself and baby Tania.

Ouma bent over as she spoke. "So many men lost their lives in the first Anglo-Boer War. My father was one, and now I may lose you." Sitting up straight she exploded, "Instead of spending so much time away from the farm at political meetings and running off to war, you should be following what's happening in the farming world." Ouma got up slowly from her chair. "Farmers are expanding, and exporting fruit to England: grapes, pears, nectarines and apples."

Miriam shook her head. Why was Ouma ranting about the farm when Dirk was about to go to war?

Dirk blocked Ouma's path as she turned to go into the house. "You've told me once before or have you forgotten. I'm aware of what's going on in farming but it takes money, and we don't have too much of that commodity to be spending it on experimenting with fruit farming. I'm telling you again we're sticking to vegetables and dairy for now."

Ouma pushed him aside. "We'll never make any money unless you're prepared to move with the times. If you were more interested in the farm you wouldn't be going to fight." She walked off in a huff but not before Miriam saw the fear in Ouma's eyes.

Dirk turned to Miriam. "I know about the efforts to perfect refrigeration methods. I've heard from other farmers that our Cape fruit is being sent by ship to England. I know Ouma's upset I'm going off to fight. When I come back we'll look into maybe planting an apple orchard. My heart is in developing this farm you know that, don't you?"

Miriam nodded, trying to hide her fear, knowing the time was drawing near for him to depart. She looked to her mother who had been silent throughout this discourse and was sitting with her hands in her lap gazing out on their land. Miriam followed her gaze. The mountains surrounding the valley were covered in a blue mist. The sun was high in the sky and not a cloud in sight. She listened to bird song coming from trees shading their stoep. A peaceful scene but for how much longer? It looked like she had better go and see about lunch as Ouma had retreated inside, and her mother had retreated inside herself. Glancing back as she walked off to the kitchen she saw the two men with their heads close together talking quietly. She had known all along that it was inevitable that Dirk would go to war. A sense of dread and unease overwhelmed her, and she had to gather herself together before going into the kitchen.

THE BATTLE AT MAGERSFONTEIN

Miriam watched Dirk finish his packing and gently lift their sleeping daughter, kissing her and placing her back in the crib. Tania opened her eyes and he gently rocked her until she fell asleep again. He took Miriam into his arms and whispered, "We're heading for the Magersfontein mountains where we'll join the Boer Generals, Cronje and Koos de la Ray." Kissing her tear stained face he murmured in her ear, "Be strong for Tania, Ouma and your mama."

Miriam was bereft of words as she followed him downstairs where a few Boer farmers were waiting for him ready to depart. The ox-wagon was loaded with guns and food for the journey to Kimberley. Standing on the stoep she waved to Dirk and watched the wagon until it was out of sight. She blew her nose and wiped away the tears before going indoors to sit awhile with Ouma and her mama. She couldn't bear the silence and their visible fear. Her legs felt like lead as she stood up and went to check on Tania. She picked her up and whispered, "Will your papa ever see you grow up?"

It was the beginning of December, 1899. Troops were ordered to dig strategic trenches in front of the Magersfontein hill. Dirk was covered in dust as he dug along with his fellow farmers.

Piet grimaced. "Why can't we just wait on top of the hill, save us bloody digging. I left the goldfields to join in the fight and didn't expect to work like a slave, expected action," he moaned.

Dirk laughed. "You should've stayed on your farm. Here comes de la Rey again, better get on with it."

Koos de la Rey stood towering above them. His voice silenced them. "The British expect us to be on top of the mountain. Carry on digging."

On the eleventh December they were ready. Dirk looked at his watch. It was four o'clock in the morning. The word was out the British were approaching. Dirk raised his head slightly above the trench and saw the Highlanders and British forces coming towards them at a fast pace. His heart raced. Six hundred metres, then five hundred metres and at four hundred metres the General gave the command to shoot. The noise was deafening. Dirk's arms felt numb. He tasted sweat. Kept blinking his eyes. Wiped his forehead. By midday, the sun was at its hottest. His throat was dry. His voice hoarse. They kept firing into line after line of British Officers throughout the day. At four o'clock in the afternoon Dirk and Piet watched British soldiers as they fled the battlefield. A few had broken through and were climbing the hill whilst others became entangled in the wire fencing. All were shot.

Dirk felt exhausted but jubilant. He looked up over the trench and saw the British doctors going to their wounded and dead. Turning to Piet he shouted. "Come, we must help them." They left their safe positions along with other Boers and went to assist the wounded enemy. British gunfire rained down on them but they carried on sharing their water and helping the wounded. Their wounded and dead were far fewer than the British. Returning to the trench he hardly slept that night. The smell of death was everywhere.

The following day he asked Piet, "What's happening?"

Piet replied, "General de la Ray has offered the British a cease fire to remove their wounded and dead."

Dirk crawled out of the trench and went to help, unheeding of Piet's warning, "They'll shoot us like they did yesterday. You can't trust them, man." But he went after Dirk. Piet heard the British Naval gun go off, firing on both Boer and British. A deafening sound breaking the silence. Dropping to the ground he watched in horror as Dirk fell forwards. His scream was drowned by the return fire of the Boers, who quickly silenced the big gun.

It was two o'clock in the afternoon on the second day when the British troops finally retreated. The Boers stood before General de la Rey. Piet's head was bowed as the General's voice reached him.

"I'm proud of our victory but also for the compassion you showed to the wounded British soldiers. For your bravery going to their assistance even though you were fired on, and to those who lost their lives in this heroic manner. They will never be forgotten. We have lost seventy one men and there are a hundred and forty-two wounded. But the British have lost far more. I congratulate you. You are extraordinary men. The British sent their finest troops, the Guards and the Highland Brigades. They called us a 'rabble of farmers.' We've shown them what a rabble can do."

A cheer went up but Piet didn't join in.

Miriam waited each day for news of Dirk. She watched Ouma Rosie slowly fade away. It seemed she lived for Dirk. Ouma expected the worst and she refused to listen to her. Hendrik had also gone to fight, so the business of the farm was left in her hands for which she was unprepared. It seemed a daunting task. She tried to get Ouma to give advice about managing the farm in order to get her involved, but Ouma wasn't interested. She had taken to walking their dog each day, regardless of her arthritis. As for her mama, Ouma simply ignored her. Miriam saw the anguish in Ouma's eyes and refrained from saying anything. She buried herself doing the book-keeping, and relied on Thembeki to look after Tania during the day, returning in the evenings to bath Tania and put her to bed.

She felt grateful to Cook. Each day after breakfast her mama would take the dishes into the kitchen and sit and talk to her. Miriam waited until Ouma went to sit on the stoep and followed her mama into the kitchen to check all was well.

"Don't you let Ouma upset you Madam," said Cook pouring Becky another cup of tea just the way she liked it, black with a slice of lemon.

Miriam helped herself to a flask of tea to take to the office and smiled as Cook refused to call her mama by her name or surname, saying that her tongue would not roll over such a long name. Through the kitchen window she caught sight of Dominee coming down the path and went to greet him.

"Dominee I'm so glad to see you. I'm on my way to the office. Could you talk to Ouma and try and cheer her up? You're the only one who can get through to her."

"Of course my dear. I'm doing the rounds, trying to bring comfort where I can."

"It's a great comfort to see you, Dominee. If it wasn't for you, we wouldn't know what was happening. I must go now but please come again soon."

"Of course I will Miriam. You know how fond I am of you all."

"Good morning, Ouma and how are you today?" Dominee sat himself down in a comfortable chair on the stoep.

"Morning, Dominee. What's good about it? I'll call Thembeki to get some tea for you."

Dominee held up his hand. "No thank you, Ouma. Tea is for the English, not me. I heard General de la Rey and Cronje have practically wiped out the English at Magersfontein."

"Ja, Dominee, and what of our men? I've heard nothing from Dirk."

"But he's miles away. How can he get a message to you? He's in the field, Ouma. You have to be patient."

"Patience is for Dominees. Besides, how is it that you've got word about the battle?"

Ignoring her remark he said, "Why don't you come to church Ouma? It may bring you some comfort."

"Don't ask me to pray now. I prayed for my son and look what happened to him."

"Ouma, we can't know the reasons why God chooses to take some men and not others."

"You mean you don't have all the answers? Does your God exist, Dominee?"

He sat in silence, cast a searching look at the night sky and answered, "I believe there is a God."

"Belief is not good enough for me. When you know, I'll come to church."

Dominee sighed. "There's been no word back from the battle about Dirk, but I've heard there have been British losses at Lady-smith, Colenso and Stormberg. Maybe Dirk has moved on to one of these areas."

Ouma was silent and looking at her he saw eyes that held fathomless sorrow. Getting nothing more out of Ouma he said goodbye and walked down the steps muttering to himself. "If only I could find the right words when I need them. God, this web of death is spreading all over our land. Help me find the strength to comfort my people."

DIRK'S BURIAL

Miriam was just coming down the stairs when she heard someone knocking at the front door. When she opened the door she took one look at Dominee and felt her knees give way. She barely heard his next words as she fell into his arms.

"Miriam, Dirk died a brave man. He is with God my dear," and found himself half carrying Miriam into the front room helping her into a chair as Ouma let out an anguished cry.

He reached out a hand to Ouma who brushed him aside and collapsed into her chair where she rocked back and forth wringing her hands. He felt at a loss to know how to comfort them.

Becky had heard Ouma cry out and taking in the scene in the front room didn't have to ask Dominee what had happened. She took Tania to the kitchen and handed her to Thembeki and managed a few words, "Bad news Cook. Please make tea and I'll get some brandy." She poured brandy for them all. "Miriam, you must drink this down please," and held the glass to Miriam's lips.

"Mama, I can't swallow. Please no more."

Becky put her arms around Miriam and together they wept.

Miriam couldn't sleep. She kept thinking that this was a punishment because of her longing for Joseph. She dragged herself out of bed each morning to see to Tania.

Tania was the image of Dirk, and each time she picked her up it was a constant reminder of what she had lost. Each morning she handed Tania over to Thembeki.

It was a relief to go for a walk and get away from a home that had taken on a cloak of mourning. She hated the black clothes worn by Ouma and her mama. She refused to wear black.

The family buried Dirk near his favourite spot, a hill overlooking the orchard. Miriam remembered Ouma always talked about knowing where to find Dirk when he was in trouble, and said he went there to think. Miriam watched neighbours from the surrounding farms line up to speak to Ouma. They approached her but their words didn't penetrate. She was carrying Tania and didn't register her cries until Thembeki came to the rescue. Miriam looked round for her mama. Where was she when she needed her most?

Piet had taken leave to attend Dirk's funeral that took place in Dominee's church, and approached Miriam. He touched her arm. "Miriam, I want you to know Dirk was a brave man. He left our safe position and with fellow Boers led the men to help the British wounded and dying, and our own, while being fired on by the British. I was proud to fight alongside him."

Miriam raised her eyes to meet his and nodded. "Thank you for coming. I'll tell my daughter about her father's bravery one day."

"I have a farm not far from here. If you need any help …"

She didn't let him finish. "Thank you but we can manage," and walked off, looking for her mama.

Dominee followed her and put his hand on her shoulder. "Miriam, I will always come when you need me. Ouma made me feel a part of this family and I can never repay her. I will do everything in my power to protect you all."

Miriam felt hot tears roll down her face, and Dominee shielded her as they walked towards the farmhouse. Thembeki was feeding Tania in the kitchen whilst Cook stirred the soup. Dominee followed Miriam where an aroma of freshly baked bread was coming from the kitchen. Miriam filled two bowls with soup and carried them to the dining room.

Dominee pointed to the bread. "Some bread please, Cook. I don't think Miriam has eaten all day. You must look after her you hear. And don't forget Ouma and Miriam's mother."

When Cook and Thembeki were cleaning up after the wake, Cook muttered half under her breath. "Who does he think he is? The Lord Almighty Himself. Like I would forget to see to Ouma and Miriam's mother."

"You mustn't talk like that, it'll bring us bad luck." Thembeki shivered even though it was a warm summer evening.

The next morning when Cook walked into her kitchen, Thembeki was already up and making tea to take to Ouma. Cook turned round speechless pointing to the door. In walked a white dove. "Get that creature out of my kitchen," she yelled.

"It looks so sad, as if it knows Master Dirk has died."

"What nonsense, it's a bird. Voetsak jou lelike ding (Get out you ugly thing)!" Cook flapped her apron vigorously as she chased the bird round the table. She tried to grab hold of its wings as its legs touched Ouma's bread, and flew back out of the door. Thembeki grinned with her back to Cook as she listened to her grumbling. She took her time walking up the stairs with Ouma's tea. The house was deathly quiet. Words of sorrow escaped from her lips. "Will we ever laugh again?" and stopped when she saw Miriam.

"Yes, Thembeki. I'll make sure of that for Tania's sake."

A week passed with Miriam continuing to invite Dominee as always for Sunday lunch. It was the only time Ouma would speak. She had withdrawn into herself, lost weight, and as hard as Miriam tried to get her to eat, she hardly ate a morsel.

"How are you Miriam?" Dominee saw dark rings under her eyes.

"The farm keeps me busy, and so does watching over Ouma and my mama."

"I wish you would come to church, Miriam."

"God is everywhere, Dominee. I don't need to go to church to find Him."

"Yes well, we all find our own path to God, so long as we don't trample the paths of others along the way, like our men defeated at Paardeberg. Four thousand of them killed. There are too few Boers to match the numbers of the British. It's not looking good. Worst of all, President Kruger has left Pretoria and gone into exile. But our Generals are still fighting. God bless them," he said wringing his hands. "Miriam, you must get a gun to protect your family."

She looked at Dominee, shaking her head. "I wouldn't know how to use one even if I wanted to."

"I heard that the British are setting up camps near railway junctions for women and children and their servants. They're burning farms and they want us Boers to starve. Why don't you come and take shelter in my church? You'll be safe and I won't let them into God's House."

Miriam frowned. "My place is here looking after Dirk's farm. I would never leave his farm to be burned. And what of the labourers? Thank you for your offer, but the answer is no."

She said goodbye to Dominee and slowly climbed the hill where she sat beside Dirk's grave and began to talk to him. "Once Papa made decisions for me and then you. Now, I must make decisions for the whole family. I'll try not to let you down Dirk, but Dominee scares me with his talk." Miriam stood with bowed head and began to say Kaddish, and when she finished she placed a stone on his grave whispering, "this prayer is a blessing for you Dirk, so that your soul may be purified before entering the World to Come." Becoming aware it was getting dark and rain clouds were gathering she slowly made her way down the hill. She could smell the rain and stepped up her pace, feeling a cool breeze on her face. "It's like you're kissing me Dirk," touching her lips with an overwhelming feeling of sorrow.

That night she placed Tania next to her in bed. In the early hours of the next morning, Miriam sat up in bed. Sleep evaded her. Her tears were for her papa and Dirk, and began to whisper to them. "Papa you had such high hopes of a better life and it was snatched away from you. Now Dirk has been cruelly snatched away from me, and we had so little time together." With a heavy heart she stroked Tania. She felt a strange sensation almost as if Dirk was in the room. She was certain she heard him say goodnight. Was she losing her mind? "Dirk, please be here when I need you. I miss you," and gathering a sleeping Tania in her arms she was overcome with grief.

The following day Miriam heard Thembeki calling for her. "Miss Miriam, Miss Miriam."

"What's wrong?" Miriam looked up from the farm's account books. She was trying to concentrate with difficulty. She kept glancing fearfully out of the window.

"Soldiers, Miss Miriam. They've been seen by some of the labourers."

"Come quick. We must get back to the farmhouse now." Miriam hitched up her skirt running as fast as she could with Thembeki gasping for breath behind her with Tania strapped to her back. Miriam heard horses whinnying and shuddered. She saw the soldiers as she rounded the corner. Horse drawn wagons had stopped in front of the house. English soldiers armed with guns stood at attention, whilst one soldier sauntered up to Miriam.

"We have orders to remove you and all the occupants on this farm."

"We're going nowhere," Miriam said trying to keep her voice steady and her hands from shaking.

"I don't wish to harm anyone as long as you do as you're told." A British soldier stood firmly in front of her with a gun at his side. "Pack some clothes for your family. We must get to the camp before nightfall." His manner was abrupt and he averted his eyes from her gaze.

Why hadn't she listened to Dominee and armed herself? "Please don't burn this farm. I'm a widow and the farm is all I have left." The soldier looked at Miriam but his eyes told her nothing. She couldn't argue against soldiers with guns.

She turned to Thembeki. "Tell Ouma and my mama to pack a suitcase each." Then she caught sight of Ouma standing on the verandah and babbling. Miriam was sure Ouma was losing her mind, whilst her mama stood rooted to the spot.

Thembeki took them gently by the hand and led them into the house. Miriam threw as many clothes into a suitcase as she could for herself and Tania. She placed Tania's doll on the top and snapped the case shut with a vengeance as tears poured down her cheeks. Dragging the suitcase down the stairs with Tania on her hip she called out to Cook to pack food in a basket for their journey. Stepping outside into the glare of the sun, she watched in horror as soldiers rough handled labourers pushing them into a wagon. She looked round but couldn't see where Thembeki and Cook had got to. Then it was their turn to get onto the wagon. Miriam clung on to Tania who was whimpering. It was then she saw Dominee running towards her.

He quickly handed a basket to Miriam and screamed, "You set fire to this farm and you will have the wrath of God upon your heads." The soldiers wanted to put him into the wagon but he fell to his knees, praying and cursing them.

"Oh, leave him," shouted the soldier in charge. "There's no room for a mad man."

"There's no room for you in God's House," screamed Dominee as the wagons rolled forwards.

THE CONCENTRATION CAMP, 1900

Miriam carried Tania followed by her mama and Ouma, as they were herded from the wagon into an open coal truck, along with other women and children. During the journey Miriam tried to shield Tanya from the stifling heat. Eventually the train rolled into a concentration camp alongside a railway siding. A sea of tents stretched before her weary eyes. They clutched belongings that they had been allowed to take with them: three mattresses, cushions, blankets, a pot and a kettle. Then they were shepherded into an empty tent. Miriam felt traumatized from watching homes being burnt, trees chopped down and sheep slaughtered on their trek. She thought about their labourers and wondered where they had been taken.

She saw a grim expression on Ouma's face whilst her mama remained silent. She placed Tania who was sleeping on Ouma's lap, and unpacked a bottle of lemonade, some bread and cheese that Thembeki had taken from their larder for them to eat. After they'd eaten she wrapped what remained of the bread and cheese with a cloth to try and keep it fresh for the next morning. Stepping out of the tent Miriam bumped into another woman.

"Oh, I'm so sorry. I didn't see you," said Miriam.

"I'm in the tent next to yours. I'm Elmarie and this is Hannelie. She's just turned eleven. She's already making friends with your little girl."

Miriam saw Elmarie's red eyes and held out her hand. "I'm Miriam and this is Tania. Would you like to meet Ouma Rosie and my mama?"

"I'd like that. It's just the two of us," said Elmarie taking Hannelie's hand.

"Who are you talking to?" asked Ouma poking her head out of the tent.

"Elmarie, Ouma. She's in the tent next to ours. Elmarie this is Ouma Rosie and my mama."

Elmarie shook hands with Ouma and Becky.

"Who is that?" Ouma pointed to Hannelie.

"My daughter Hannelie."

"Sorry state of affairs if you ask me. To be alone with a child in this god forsaken place," mumbled Ouma.

"Elmarie is not alone anymore Ouma. We'll help each other, won't we Elmarie?"

Elmarie nodded and looked at Ouma who had a disgruntled look on her face.

"I'd better get back to my tent and sort out a few things," said Elmarie turning to go and holding out her hand to Hannelie.

"Ma, can't I stay and play with Tania?"

Miriam smiled. "Tania would love to have a friend to play with Hannelie."

"You can stay a little while. I'm sure you're all tired after a long journey. Hannelie, I'm in the next tent. Don't get lost you hear."

"I'll bring her back, don't worry Elmarie."

"Thank you Miriam. I'm so glad we've met. My husband is fighting and I'm so worried. Is your husband fighting?"

Miriam spoke softly, "My husband was killed at Magersfontein Elmarie."

"I'm so sorry Miriam. I hate this war and what it's doing to our people and country."

Summer rolled into winter and winter to summer. The beauty of autumn and spring were lost to Miriam. Life was now an endless struggle to survive. She watched Tania constantly in case she wandered off and got lost in the maze of tents. Row upon row of white tents in every direction. Dust turned to mud and back again to dust. It got into everything whilst the African sun beat down relentlessly when the weather turned. Trees so abundant on their farm were non-existent here and the heat went right through their worn shoes. She was thankful there was fresh clean water, although this was also in short supply.

"Miriam, go get your mama a little water. She needs to drink more," Ouma insisted.

Miriam felt helpless seeing her mama fade away before her very eyes. In the heat of summer, the air inside their tent was stifling, and feeling she couldn't breathe she stepped outside with Tania to get some water.

Elmarie was doing some washing and stood up rubbing her back. "How is your mama, Miriam?"

"Not good. I'm worried. She barely eats anything and clothes hang on her."

Elmarie wiped her hands on her apron. "I'm worried about Hannelie. I think she has a fever."

"Has the doctor been to see her?"

Elmarie sighed. "What's the good. What can he do?"

"Take Hannelie to see him Elmarie. It's better than worrying. I must go and get some water for Mama. Is there anything I can do for you?"

Elmarie shook her head and Miriam hugged her.

When she returned Ouma took her aside. "We must get the doctor to see your mama."

Miriam had been avoiding what was only too evident, her mother's sunken eyes and yellowing skin. She handed Tania to Ouma and feeling guilty rushed out to find the doctor.

Becky's breathing had become more shallow and Ouma put her ear to Becky's mouth, and sank back in the chair. She was still breathing. Miriam returned with the doctor. Ouma was trying to give Becky a sip of water but it dribbled down her chin.

"She won't need water old woman, not where she's going." A young man stood at the entrance of the tent.

"And you know where she's going do you? Well, it's your duty to see she stays here," said Ouma.

Miriam frowned and thought he had no bedside manner for a doctor. He was very young and maybe not experienced. Her eyes took in his polished boots. In a camp where the only thing plentiful was dust, they wouldn't remain shiny for long.

The doctor examined Becky and turned to Miriam speaking softly. "Your mother is dying."

"So, what are you now, God? You doctors think …" Ouma was stopped by Miriam putting a finger to her mouth.

"Ouma, please let me sit with my mama for the little time she has left. Can you look after Tania for me?"

"No time left for us to become friends now," said Ouma shaking her head and walked out holding Tania's hand.

Miriam bent down and kissed her mama as she slipped in and out of consciousness.

"I'm sorry. There's nothing more I can do to help your mother," said the doctor.

Becky opened her eyes and tightened her grip on Miriam's hand.

Miriam leaned over close to Becky's face. "Avraham," Becky whispered in a rasping breath.

Miriam frowned and turned to where her mother was looking but saw nothing. "Mama, it's me not Papa. Please don't leave me," she whispered between sobs. She heard a rattling sound as her mother drew her last breath.

The doctor gently released her hand still clutching her mother's, and went to fetch Ouma who put her arms around Miriam, kissed her and turned to Tania. "Come and say goodbye to Grandma Becky," gently lifting Tania up.

"There's no Rabbi to bury Mama," Miriam cried.

"Your prayers will be enough Miriam," said Ouma.

They buried Becky in a graveyard in the open veld amidst all the other graves, and Miriam said a prayer. Ouma Rosie followed her daughter-in-law's lead throwing soil onto the grave. They walked slowly back to the camp.

"Where's Grandma Becky?" Tania asked tugging on Ouma Rosie's hand.

"She's gone to be with Grandpa Avraham," said Ouma avoiding Miriam's questioning look.

Miriam knew only too well that all Ouma believed in was their land. Now all that was left was Ouma and Tania. She had to make certain they returned to their land.

One day rolled into the next and Ouma spat as she spotted the doctor coming towards them, raising her voice. "There's not enough water for us to drink. You English should be ashamed of yourselves. Look at all the sick and dying in this camp."

The doctor stopped mid-stride. "That's exactly why I've come. Your neighbour has a very sick child. At least you have clean water in this camp. Reports have gone to Parliament on the problems in the camps."

"Talk, talk, talk. That's all it is. Send me to your Parliament and I'll tell them what we need. We need to return to our farms, that's if you haven't burned them all to the ground. We need proper rations. Becky was a skeleton before we buried her." Ouma spat. "You think we can survive on a little flour, sugar, coffee and salt. We only eat meat three times a week. You call that a full ration! Our children only get a half ration, not enough for a mouse to survive. My granddaughter is fading away before my very eyes and yours, if you'll only look."

Miriam was too tired to put a stop to Ouma's rant, and shut her eyes not wanting to look at the ribs protruding from Tania's little body.

"None of this is of my doing," said the doctor flinching under Ouma's harsh stare and started to walk off.

"Don't you walk away. I haven't finished talking to you yet," she shouted as he disappeared into Elmarie's tent.

"Ouma, there's a rumour that a Miss Emily Hobhouse has visited our camp."

"Who is Emily Hobhouse?" asked Ouma.

"She's a British welfare campaigner and she's trying to improve our lives in the camp. They say she's brought supplies with her," said Miriam feeling her shoulders sag from fatigue.

Ouma stood with hands on hips. "I hope that'll be before any more of us die. If I'd seen her I would have told her exactly what I think."

"Ouma, if you didn't give the doctor and officers a hard time they would give us more meat and rice. Look how thin you're getting."

"Well, I don't like rice. What do they think, we're Chinese? Boere folk eat meat."

"At least the doctor has increased the ration for Tania." All she wanted to do was lie down and sleep. Instead Ouma's voice was like someone constantly beating a drum.

"She's a growing child, how can it be enough? You must try and get more food for Tania. I don't want her ending up in their hospital."

"Ouma, children are dying of measles and typhus fever. If their mothers allowed them to go to hospital they might not die." She thought of Elmarie who wouldn't hear of Hannalie being moved to the hospital. It meant she had to keep Tania from going into Elmarie's tent for fear her daughter would also succumb.

The daily struggle for survival carried on, and she felt exhausted battling with Ouma to stop offending the camp officers. But Ouma continued to speak her mind no matter the consequence, which meant no meat for them until she stopped her tirades. Finally Ouma looked the other way when the doctor or officials came past. They sat huddled in their cramped tent that winter. The rain came in under the tent flaps and their mattresses became soaked. All around children lay sick on the ground, emaciated and lifeless.

Miriam stood outside Elmarie's tent and called out softly, "Elmarie, how is Hannelie?" Elmarie opened the tent flap. "Hanneli is no better Miriam, and before you say anything, I'm not going to let the doctor put her into hospital. Do you know how many sick children are lying in that hospital?"

Miriam shook her head and didn't want to know. She couldn't bear to see Elmarie cry.

Ouma prodded her. "Miriam, take some of our rations to Elmarie for Hannelie. Elmarie looks gaunt and that child hasn't been out of the tent for days now."

"It's too late for Hannelie, Ouma."

"Nonsense, you take them some food now." Ouma hauled herself up and put some bread on a plate.

"Ouma, stop that. If we had more I'd be willing to share but we don't. I have to think about Tania."

"Didn't you talk about helping each other? You haven't seen

much of Elmarie have you?"

"Don't look at me like that. Hannelie is a sick child and I don't want Tania coming into contact with her."

"I'm not judging you," said Ouma shrugging.

"Yes, you are," and Miriam put the food back.

The Captain of their camp was sympathetic and started to distribute more warm clothing.

"Ouma, we heard that Emily Hobhouse has spoken about our suffering in England, and collected money to help us, that's why we've been given warm clothing."

"Too late for Hannelie. The child is skin and bone," replied Ouma staring straight ahead.

Miriam knew Ouma would never forgive the English.

Miriam listened to Ouma talking to Tania about the taste of warm roast chicken and koeksisters that melted in the mouth. "I can smell chicken roasting in the oven," said Ouma sipping some water and spitting it out. "Disgusting, not like the pure water from our reservoir."

Miriam sighed. Life was hard enough without Ouma's constant grumbling. She had to take on all their chores as Ouma didn't have the strength to help anymore.

Ouma sat watching Miriam doing the washing. "That water, it's as dirty as those clothes. Waste of time trying to keep clean in this hell."

Miriam ignored her. She felt better occupying her time. Endless time that dragged on day after day. Her one delight was Tania who loved to help and would hand her clothes to hang up to dry. Sometimes they would fall onto dusty ground but Miriam didn't have the heart to scold her. She would give them a shake, and see the smile Ouma gave her granddaughter that seldom graced her face these days.

"It'll be a miracle if they're not stolen," Ouma announced as loudly as she could sitting guard outside their tent. Miriam shook her head at Ouma hoping no one had heard.

"I'm going to get our rations Ouma."

"See if you can get a bit extra for Hannelie while you're about it."

Miriam stood outside Elmarie's tent holding Tania's hand afraid to go inside and called out. "Elmarie, I'm going to get our rations. Would you like me to get yours?"

Elmarie popped her head outside the tent. "Thank you Miriam."

The doctor had been kind to Miriam ever since her mama died. He always saw to it that there were extra rations for Tania. She could only try to get a little extra for Hannelie. This time he told her, "The Boers and English are meeting at Vereeniging to negotiate peace. But you can't return home yet. You'll have nothing to return to and you'll end up starving."

"We're starving here. How much worse could it be? What do you mean nothing to return to? What about our farm?" She stared at him feeling bewildered.

He didn't look her in the eye as he spoke. "Lord Milner said the camps have been a mistake."

"What?" Miriam hardly believing what she'd just heard. He actually admitted they were a mistake. She thought about what lay ahead. Would they have a house to return to? Each day it was the thought of returning to their farm that kept her from giving up. She didn't stay to hear any more, collected their rations and made her way back to their tent. She kept repeating to herself. "A mistake, they call this uprooting of a nation, a mistake." Arriving at their tent she blurted out. "They call our camp a mistake Ouma."

Ouma frowned. "They'll have to pay dearly for their mistake. Who told you?"

"Heard it from the doctor's mouth."

"You must find out what's happening to our menfolk. Talk nicely to him."

"What do you mean talk nicely? He's no friend."

"No, but hasn't he given us more rations for Tania. He likes you Miriam. Maybe, he'll tell you more."

Miriam went straight to Elmarie and gave her the rations. "I managed to get a little more for Hannelie." She didn't tell Elmarie that she'd taken a little extra from their rations for Hannelie.

"Thank you Miriam. I'm so tired. Hannelie's not getting any better."

"Why don't you let the doctor treat her in the hospital?"

Elmarie shook her head. "No, I can look after her better myself."

"I'll collect your rations for you."

Elmarie hugged her and Miriam could see she couldn't speak. "It's no trouble Elmarie."

Each day Miriam went to look for the doctor. She didn't even know his name. She would try to be nice. But when she finally found him in one of the tents serving as a surgery he took advantage fondling her breasts and she shrank back. She tried not to show how repulsed she felt. He was key to Tania and their survival.

"I thought you liked me?"

Miriam replied. "Yes, but not like that." It didn't stop him from forcefully kissing her. She felt nauseated. She had to get out but he barred her way. His hand went under her skirt, up her thigh. He pushed her towards the bed. She was shaking as she tried to scream but his hand was firmly over her mouth. His weight was on her when the tent flap opened.

"What the bloody hell is going on here?" demanded the Captain of their camp.

Miriam didn't look back and ran as fast as she could and fell into Ouma's arms. Ouma held her gently as Miriam out of breath tried to find the words to tell Ouma what had happened.

Tania kept asking. "Why's Mama crying?" and when she didn't get an answer put her arms around her mother like Ouma was doing.

Shortly afterwards Miriam went with Ouma to listen to a former Boer general, Piet de Wet, who came to the camp to talk to the women. He tried to convince them to pressurize their husbands to surrender their arms. Miriam saw him look directly at one Boer woman, a Mrs Botha, for support. She shook her head and turned her back on him and walked to her tent in silence. She was followed by Miriam and all the other women with Ouma spitting out the words. "The foul turncoat."

It was early morning when Miriam first heard an anguished cry coming from Elmarie's tent. She ran to see what was wrong dreading what she'd find. It was what she suspected. She sat in silence with Elmarie beside Hannelie who was dying.

The mourners were allowed ten minutes for the funeral service. They huddled together outside Elmarie's tent. Psalm 103:8 was sung by two Boer women and they said a prayer. "Our brief life is like grass. Like a flower in the field." Another prayer followed for Elmarie who had given up her child as so many had done.

Elmarie's voice broke as she sobbed. "Hannelie is with God now."

Miriam put her arm around her as they made their way towards the graveyard. She walked on Elmarie's right and another woman on her left keeping Elmarie from collapsing.

The fear of death was a black shadow that hovered over all the women with children in the camp. So many were dying of disease and malnutrition.

It was May 1902. They were called before a camp official who said he wished to make an announcement. Rumours had spread that they would have to accept King Edward VII as their Sovereign when the war ended.

"Never," hissed Ouma and spat in disgust. "Dominee's God has forsaken us."

Standing before all the women and children with a paper in his hand he proceeded to read. "The Treaty of Vereeniging was signed on the 31st day of May, 1902. The war is over. You and your menfolk will be helped to return to your homes and farms. You'll receive money to rebuild and re-stock your farms." He turned and walked away.

Ouma held on to Tania's hand as she turned to Miriam. "Will we have a farm to go back to? Will our home still be there?" her voice trembled.

"Ouma, we'll rebuild if we have to." She didn't want to admit that she was afraid of what they might find when they returned home.

Elmarie came to say goodbye. "Miriam, I've had word that my husband is on his way to collect me."

"I'm so happy for you Elmarie. Will you go back to your home?"

Elmarie shrugged, "I don't know if we'll have a home to go back to?"

Miriam nodded for she didn't dare think there might be no home for her family to return to.

The train rolled forward homeward bound this time and Miriam thought she felt her mama's presence and hugged Tania. She glanced back and the last thing she saw before closing her eyes was her mama's grave, and then it was gone in a cloud of dust. When they transferred to a horse drawn wagon the horses picked up speed on the last of the trek home. There was silence as they witnessed the scorched earth policy and saw burnt out farms and homes. Tears rolled down Miriam's face as she shielded Tania's eyes from the devastation, and felt Ouma reach out to hold her hand.

THE HOMECOMING

Dominee stood at the end of the drive waiting. It was midday. He had been there every day since receiving news that the women and children would be returned to their homes. Those who had homes to return to. Thembeki brought him a glass of water.

"Dominee, why don't you come inside and wait?" She noticed dark rings under his eyes and greying hair. He had aged. Then she heard him shout.

"They're coming," and he fell to his knees in prayer.

A wagon slowly drew near pulled by four horses. Thembeki just made out the figures of two women and a small child and began to run as the wagon drew to a halt. Ouma reached out and almost tumbled into Thembeki's outstretched arms.

Thembeki stood back admiring Tania. "Oh Miss Miriam, we prayed for your return. Tania, you're such a big girl and so pretty. But, Miss Miriam, where is your mama?"

Miriam's tears were a mixture of joy and sorrow. "She didn't make it. I wish we could have buried my mama next to Dirk."

"Oh, Miss Miriam I'm so sorry. I was fond of your mama and so was Cook," and put her arms around Miriam.

Then a little voice piped up. "Where's the dog?" Thembeki kneeled and took Tania's hand and they walked towards Dominee. "You'll see," she said in a choked voice.

Ouma fell into Dominee's arms and then he hugged Miriam. He couldn't stop the tears running down his cheeks.

"Dominee, what's left of the house?" Miriam asked anxiously.

"Take a look down the avenue," without another word he lifted Tania up so that she could also see. His smile broadened as she studied his face with interest and pulled his beard. He put her down gently.

"Dominee, we heard all our homes were burned to the ground. We didn't know if we'd have a home to return to," said Miriam casting her eyes in the direction of their home.

"I told the soldiers if they set fire to your house, they would have to set fire to me," and he laughed.

"What happened to our farm labourers?"

"Well, I managed to save Thembeki and Cook. Hid them in the church. Told the soldiers they were only allowed in God's House if they came to pray."

"You mean Cook is here too?" Ouma's face lit up.

Miriam was amused. She had only ever seen the two of them bickering.

Together they walked slowly along the avenue towards their farmhouse. The wagon followed behind them. Tania skipped for joy when she saw Rusty coming towards them. Cook stood by the stoep and Miriam stood to the side as Cook hugged Ouma gently and then gave Tania a huge smile. Thembeki whispered in Cook's ear and Cook hugged Miriam with tears in her eyes. "Miss Miriam, I'll miss your mama." Miriam nodded, unable to reply as she looked at the farmhouse that she thought she would never see again. The grass was dry and long and the flower beds overgrown with weeds but she was overjoyed to see that their home was still standing. She was anxious to see inside and was impatient waiting for Ouma who was walking slowly. Walking into the sitting room, she picked up a picture of Dirk. The glass was shattered. She replaced it on the mantelpiece. There were few pieces of furniture left and curtains were torn. Dominee helped Ouma sit down. Miriam trembled as she looked at the bare remains of a house they had once been so proud of.

"Will you stay with Ouma, Dominee? I want to have a look at the barn. Thembeki will you look after Tania for a little while?"

Thembeki smiled at Tania who took her hand and the two went off with Rusty following. Miriam couldn't bear to look at Ouma's stricken face. She walked briskly and stopped for a moment preparing for the worst. Peering inside the barn she could see it had been emptied of all its contents except for a lawnmower. The trapdoor suddenly flew open. She looked up and peering down at her was the face of a young black boy.

"What are you doing there?" Miriam took a step backwards. The young boy took out a ladder and climbed down.

"Miss, Thembeki and Cook said I'd be safe here."

"What's your name?"

"Michael, Miss"

"Where are your ma and pa?"

"They were taken in the wagon when the soldiers came. My ma made me run and Thembeki brought me here to hide Miss."

Miriam's voice softened. "Well, you're safe now but you can't stay here." He shivered in his thin, torn shirt. The cold seeped through every crevice in the barn and the wind made a howling noise through the cracks in the roof.

Miriam looked at his anxious face. "There'll be lots of jobs for you to do. Thembeki and Cook will find a place for you to stay.

Come, follow me."

"My ma and pa Miss, did they come back with you?"

"No. But we'll ask Cook if she's heard any news."

She walked on and Michael wiped his tears on his torn sleeve.

Cook prepared vegetable soup and home baked bread. Only that morning she and Thembeki had picked fresh vegetables from a small vegetable patch that they kept going with the help of Michael. She sent Thembeki into the cellar for some wine. The cellar door had remained undiscovered. It had been hidden from view by a screen covered in cobwebs. The house had been ransacked but Dominee had saved it from being razed to the ground in the "Scorched Earth" Policy. Thembeki and Cook had cleared the house of dust and cobwebs and cleaned till their backs ached.

Thembeki helped Ouma to sit and soon they were enjoying Cook's homemade bean soup and bread. Dominee poured the wine this time and Miriam had to hide a smile as Ouma said nothing. It seemed like old times to Miriam except for the two empty chairs at their table.

Dominee raised his glass, "To your homecoming and the future."

Miriam raised her glass, "To you Dominee. You've been a part of this family for so long. I'd be honoured if you'll be Tania's godfather."

"I will have to ask Tania first." He looked at her with a twinkle in his eye.

"I'd like a Papa." She smiled up at him and put her hand in his.

He sniffed, let go of Tania's hand and took a handkerchief out of his pocket. Wiped his glasses and took her hand in his again.

Time passed and it seemed that life returned to normal. The tradition of Sunday lunch resumed. Ouma closed her eyes breathing in the delicious smell of roast chicken. She was on her second helping when she noticed Tania pushing her food around her plate and just eating vegetables.

"You eat that chicken young lady otherwise you'll go hungry, as we all did in the camp."

Tania pushed her plate away. "I'm not eating chicken." Crossing her arms she glared at Ouma.

Miriam sighed. "Tania, I promised you Cook won't harm your pet chicken. Now listen to Ouma and be grateful we have enough food for all of us to eat."

"How can you make such a promise to the child," Ouma bellowed.

"Don't worry Ouma. We have plenty hens in the coup."

"Why does she have to have a hen as a pet?" Ouma threw her hands up in the air and looked at Dominee. "What do you say?"

He swallowed a piece of chicken and almost choked on it. Coughing and spluttering he replied, "It's just a phase Ouma. She'll grow out of it."

"Is that all you can say?" Ouma shook her head. "She's got you wound round her little finger."

"Let's have some tea on the stoep," said Miriam getting up from the table. Life had returned to normal with Ouma back to her old self. Together with Dominee they helped Ouma sit in a chair facing away from the sun.

"Oh, that's wonderful. I can feel the warm sun kissing my back," and Ouma sat back relaxing.

After lunch Dominee read the newspaper and Tania played with her doll beside him. Rusty lay snoring in a sunny spot. Dominee's glasses slipped to the end of his nose.

"Dominee, you look troubled. What is it?" Ouma asked concerned.

He read aloud. "Ai, Ouma, it says here that thousands of lives have been lost in the war. Twenty two thousand British soldiers. Six thousand to seven thousand Boer soldiers. And listen to this, twenty-thousand to twenty-eight thousand Boer civilians. They don't even know how many black Africans lost their lives and think maybe about twenty thousand?"

"And, what about our poor womenfolk. Many of their men were sent away as prisoners of war. How are they to survive?" Ouma demanded.

Miriam poured the tea and sat down. "I heard our men were sent to prisoner of war camps in St Helena, Ceylon (Sri Lanka), Bermuda, India and even Portugal."

"War is a tragedy. The British are recompensing us to the sum of three million pounds to rebuild and restock our farms. They promise us eventual self-government," said Dominee putting his newspaper down and lifting Tania onto his lap. She pulled his glasses off his nose giggling with delight. "Our men are returning slowly," he said retrieving his glasses.

"Some may never return Dominee," Miriam shook her head.

"We'll help these women and support them," he replied.

"We'll help when we're back on our feet, Dominee," Ouma's voice was gruff.

"We have to plant crops to sell to the markets and shops. We'll have to start all over again." Ouma sighed. "I feel so tired."

"War is a travesty. Why can't people negotiate to begin with then we could prevent all this loss of life," said Dominee refilling his glass.

"That's a good question and I would have thought you, a man of God, would have the answer," said Ouma.

Dominee remained silent. Then spoke so quietly Ouma strained to hear him. "War is man's doing. I preach goodwill to all men, black and white. Try to reach out a helping hand to my neighbour in the good Christian tradition. But power and greed get in the way."

"You're a good man, Dominee. Perhaps I'll come to a Sunday service one day," said Ouma smiling.

Dominee smiled. "You'll make me a very happy man Ouma if you'll give God a chance."

"Hmm, I would have thought it's the other way around. I'm going to lie down now. Miriam help me up."

Miriam could tell she was in pain. Ouma walked slowly holding on to her. She led her to a room downstairs as Ouma couldn't manage the stairs any longer.

Dominee held out his hand to Tania and Rusty followed as they walked towards the hen house. "Let's go see this hen of yours."

♣ ♣ ♣

The money the British gave them helped to buy essentials for the farm, and Miriam put what money she could aside to replace what had been broken or burnt. There had been no money left for curtaining and she pointed out to Ouma that the shutters would do for the time being. They kept the house cool in summer. Ouma's wish for velvet curtains was a luxury they couldn't afford.

"Dominee said the Boer prisoners of war were sent to other countries. The war is over so what's happened to our men?" Thembeki gazed out of the kitchen window half hoping for a miracle.

Cook stood with her back to Thembeki and turned round with tears streaking down her face. "I spoke to some of our men. They told me there were about sixty camps for us blacks. They didn't have enough food and many died of disease and hunger. I don't know if I'll ever see my man again. They say the British have done nothing to make our lives better."

"I'm sorry Cook. I shouldn't have said anything. Sit down and I'll make you a cup of tea."

"Tea may warm my belly Thembeki, but who will warm my bed again?"

Just then Dominee and Tania walked past the kitchen on the way to see her pet hen. Tania waved and called out to Thembeki. "I'm going to see my friends, bye."

Thembeki waved back and Cook got up as quick as a rocket going off. "Hey, Dominee," she shouted, but he walked on deep in conversation with Tania.

"I can see trouble ahead. What if I pick the wrong hen to roast?! Dominee only has ears for that child. Since he became her papa he's more here than at his church. You'd think Tania was his daughter."

"Ag shame on you, Cook. Leave the poor man alone. What other pleasures does he have in his life?"

"I could think of one, the watering hole. People talk you know.

I heard Dominee was told there were lots of lost souls in the watering hole. That's why he went in the first place until he nearly lost his soul to the booze. Now the rumour goes that Dominee walks right past with Tania and Rusty. Dominee was asked if he just takes 'tea' now, but pretended he hadn't heard."

"Cook, if it wasn't for Dominee we might not be here today."

"As long as he remembers who is boss here." Cook closed her eyes and sipped the tea.

~ ~ ~

It was the year 1914 and Dominee came by often to see how they were getting on with planting potatoes and vegetables. Almost half their workforce had made it back after the war. Miriam counted themselves fortunate. She had met fellow farmers at the market who had far fewer labourers. She wanted to improve their lot and huts were built for their families. When the men returned they helped rebuild their homes. She began to rely more and more on Michael who did whatever job was asked of him.

Ouma was sitting and reading and holding the book close to her eyes.

"You need glasses Ouma," said Miriam.

"Ag, leave me alone. I can see fine."

Tania perked up. "You're always nagging Ouma."

"Quite right." Ouma patted Tania's hand. "That money you're spending on huts could be invested in the farm."

"Ouma, I am investing in the farm. If our labourers are happy, they'll work harder and we won't lose them to any neighbouring farms. They're all looking for strong men."

"Our nearest neighbour is Piet and he doesn't want any of our labourers, he wants a wife. You're a young woman and have years ahead of you. I don't want you to have the life I did when Dirk's Pa died. Do you want to end up a lonely old woman?"

"Ouma, stop worrying about me. I have Tania, you and Dominee and one day I'll hand over a successful farm to Tania."

"Who says I want to be a farmer?" said Tania.

"You're too young to know what you want," said Miriam.

"I want to go to university," declared Tania.

"When you finish school Tania, we'll talk about it." Miriam looked away and sighed.

"You never listen to what I want?" said Tania standing up.

Miriam felt a headache coming on and then Ouma started.

"I won't be around for ever Miriam, nor will Dominee. We're getting old in case you hadn't noticed. This farm needs a man. I've asked Piet for Sunday lunch."

"A man!" Miriam exclaimed. "Since I've taken over the running of this farm have you gone hungry? Besides which I have Hendrik to help me. I don't need another man."

"Hmf. A young woman needs a man. That's all I can say," muttering under her breath, "preferably one who isn't married."

How could Ouma know how she felt about Hendrik? She changed the subject, "I've heard from other farmers at the market that farmers are shipping fruit in refrigerators to England."

"Ja? They're successful farmers. If you follow their example, like I once advised Dirk, then maybe we can also be successful."

Miriam felt beads of sweat break out on her forehead and her headache was worsening. "What do you mean by that?"

"Well, these farmers had a vision. Do you have a vision for our farm?"

"I've been following developments. I'm quite capable of taking this farm into the future."

Ouma got up with Tania's help. "You're such a blessing Tania. Remember Miriam, Tania will be more use to you with a good education," and winking at Tania she shuffled off down the path.

Miriam took a slow walk to the office stopping to watch the sheep grazing, and the labourers tilling the soil checking for potato moths and fungis. She felt a sense of pride and fulfilment in what they had achieved. She thought back to the days in the Schtetl and to life on the farm. There was only one thing missing and that was Dirk beside her to reap the benefits of their hard work. An image of

Joseph emerged as he always did when a feeling of loneliness descended upon her. "Perhaps it is fate," she murmured aloud as her thoughts turned to Hendrik who had become indispensable to her.

"Did you say something?" Hendrik was standing waiting for her. Their hands touched as he took the books from her.

Miriam smiled up at him. "Just thinking aloud. We're not doing too badly you know. Maybe there'll be a little money to pay a teacher for our labourer's children."

"You're serious aren't you? But you'll have to pass it by Ouma, and you know what she'll say."

"Oh yes, and what will that be?"

"That this farm is not a charity and the money could be better spent on expanding into other areas of farming."

"Mmm, well Ouma can say what she likes. I'm going to find a teacher for the children. Their nearest school is miles away and they can't walk so far every day in all kinds of weather." She looked at Hendrik thoughtfully. "I'm thinking of planting an apple orchard and I've been talking to other farmers in the area. But it can wait. Right now we've a deadline to get our produce to the market in on time.

Hendrik nodded. "I've got wooden boxes for packing and managed to get the railway timetable."

Together they examined the timetable and their outlets in Cape Town. Miriam felt happy that business was picking up and the farm was at last showing a profit. She depended on Hendrik. But, more than that she could tell by the way he looked at her that there was a growing attraction between them.

At the end of the day Miriam put the books away. Hendrik had left early and she locked the office, and walked slowly up towards the hill and sat down beside Dirk's grave. The silence broken only by birdsong. She breathed in the fresh, crisp evening air, and placed a few daisies on Dirk's grave with thoughts crowding her mind. She would have to fight Ouma before she could make any changes. She would have listened to you, Dirk, but Ouma thinks a farm needs a man's hand. We had so little time together. Then the past came rushing back. Joseph slipped into her thoughts. Did he ever think about her? She was forty-four and still Joseph was a fixture in her head and heart. If she kept looking back she'd be frozen in the past and wouldn't be able to move on. Tania was growing up and seemed to have inherited Dirk's stubbornness. She wanted to go to university when she finished school, but was needed on the farm. Ouma and Dominee of course were on Tania's side. What else did she expect? Tania could do no wrong in their eyes. She wished Dirk was around to advise her. She didn't dare voice her thoughts about Hendrik. It seemed indecent to think about him at Dirk's grave. She wanted a man by her side but also in her bed. She got up with a sigh and made her way back to the farmhouse.

The lights of the farmhouse were a welcome sight. The trees they had planted had grown tall and offered shade from the intense heat in the summer. She cherished the peace they now enjoyed, and thought about Dominee's news of the rebellion by the Afrikaner republicans to regain political and national independence lost in 1902. They had been unsuccessful and many lost their lives. Would war always be a malevolent shadow. Dominee frightened her with his talk of men going to fight alongside their allies in the First World War. Yet another war. She glanced up at dark clouds gathering above. Picking up her skirt she ran for cover as the heavens opened with the crash of thunder.

In the days that followed Dominee and Miriam worked side by side harvesting a small crop of potatoes and vegetables. Miriam wiped the sweat from her brow. She looked at Dominee who seemed to be struggling in the heat.

"Let's take a break. I've brought some of Cook's biscuits and lemonade. You don't have to be doing this Dominee. You have a congregation to serve."

"It's a welcome relief from my work and I love the smell of God's earth."

Walking slowly they sat down under the welcome shade of a tree. Miriam poured some lemonade for them both.

"Why do we have to get involved in this war?" she asked leaning against a tree trunk and watching a herd of cows grazing peacefully in the nearby field.

Dominee wiped his mouth with his sleeve. "Because we've offered Britain military and financial support."

Miriam shook her head. "It wasn't long ago the British put us in concentration camps and burned our land and farms. And now we're friends?"

Hendrick came up behind them and chipped in. "South Africa's interests are better served by a future within the British Empire." He smiled at Miriam and sat down beside her.

She knew what he had come to tell her. "You're going to fight aren't you?" She felt her body sag. "I'm forty-four and have hair turning grey with worry."

Hendrik grasped her hands in his. "You're strong and beautiful Miriam. You'll come through this war. I'm not so sure I will."

"Then why go? I need you," she ignored Dominee's frown. Time was precious now and she no longer cared what anyone thought. "All this talk of war upsets Ouma. I need every pair of hands for harvesting and depend on you Hendrik." She felt herself tremble with the magnitude of what lay ahead for her.

"There's a call to arms now. Anyone working on a farm is seen as avoiding call up. You won't be able to hide me."

"How will I manage without you Hendrik?"

Dominee got up slowly. "Ahem, I'll leave the two of you and pray for you my dear."

"I need strong men Dominee, prayers won't help me." Feeling guilty she added, "Go see Ouma. She's in bed today."

"Is she ill?" asked Dominee.

"No, like I said, the talk of war upsets her. Please go to her." Miriam desperately wanted to be alone with Hendrik.

Dominee nodded and walked off slowly to her relief. Miriam knew she had no right to Hendrik. He was a married man, but the thought of him going to war frightened her. It was hard to hide how she felt about him and she couldn't help gazing at him with longing. She didn't resist when he pulled her towards him, covering her face with kisses, until she laughed and lay down on the soft green grass. He caressed her gently and Miriam responded. She could think of nothing else but her need for Hendrik. She took a deep breath as they lay in each other's arms. "I want you Hendrik."

"Are you sure about this Miriam?"

Miriam got up and reached out her hand. "Come, no one will disturb us in my bedroom. I don't want to waste another minute before you leave to fight."

"You talk as if I'm not going to return from war."

The front door was open and Miriam held her breath as they passed Ouma who was with Dominee. She led Hendrik quietly up the stairs to her bedroom and closed the door. He wrapped her in his arms and she responded with a passion she'd held at bay for so long.

"Why must we fight in Africa?" Ouma pulled her shawl tighter across her chest.

Dominee noticed a slight tremor of her hands before she placed them under the shawl. He frowned and looked up. "Britain has to keep shipping lanes open, and Germany's ports in her African colonies are a threat."

"Hmf, you know what I think of Britain after our Boer War. Cook tells me that our labourers are being used as carriers. They're given little to eat and march in rain and searing heat. Who will protect us Boers?"

"Botha, Ouma. He believes we can beat the Germans. These Colonels are intelligent men."

"Is that so? It takes greater intelligence to bring opposing sides to the negotiating table. Like your Bible says, 'when swords shall be made into ploughshares,' you should know you're the preacher."

"I'm impressed you remember something of your church going

days," Dominee said with a hint of a smile.

"War is damnable and you'd think your God hadn't given men tongues to speak."

"Why blame God Ouma? It's men who incite war."

"Well, I've had enough. No one can disturb me when I'm dead and buried." She closed her eyes and sank onto her pillows.

Dominee rose realising he was being dismissed, and left closing the door quietly. Ouma opened one eye and poured herself a glass of wine. "If I'm to die, I shall have the best wine to ease my way into the next world. Only my dreams disturb me. I don't understand them. Maybe I should talk to Miriam. She wouldn't laugh at me would she?" Ouma muttered to herself and finished the wine.

The house was quiet as Dominee left shielding his eyes from the sun and then spotted Tania. "Where are you off to in such a hurry? No time to talk to Papa?"

She gave him a hug. "I must go help with the harvest. Even Cook and Thembeki are helping now and some of our labourers' wives."

"I'll walk with you," said Dominee keeping an eye open for Miriam and Hendrik on the way. When they got to the field the women were carrying baskets filled with vegetables on their heads but there was no sign of Hendrik or Miriam. He nodded as he passed the women too hot to remove his hat. "Thank God the drought hasn't destroyed the crop. I feel closest to God here," he said listening to the women sing as they worked. The hens scrambled around them for insects and Dominee turned to Tania. "What happened to your pet hen? Did we eat her at Christmas time?" he asked with a twinkle in his eye.

"You're a tease Papa, and I'm grown up now." Tania laughed digging out the few remaining potatoes. Some were shrivelled up from lack of water.

"Sixteen is grown up now? I expect you have other interests now, like a boyfriend?"

Tania blushed and burst out, "He goes to your church Papa."

"A good lad then."

"He's Jan's son, Adam."

"Hmm, comes from a good family," nodding approvingly. "Do your ma and Ouma know?"

"Of course. He's been invited to Sunday lunch."

"Ah, then Ouma must approve."

Miriam followed the news of the war that continued to filter through and was recorded in the newspapers. That Sunday, a solemnity filled the dining room. Food was scarce but Cook had prepared a feast in everyone's eyes. The smell of roast chicken pervaded the house. It was brought through by Thembeki together with roast potatoes. Dessert followed with koeksisters and tea.

Dominee took a deep breath and raised his voice above the sounds of Adam eating. "Bandawe, a Theologian, said slave-dealing was carried out by Portuguese policemen."

Adam stopped chewing. "Who is Bandawe? Never heard of him."

"His tribe's from Nyasaland and made to do forced labour growing cotton."

"What happened to them?" asked Tania helping Adam to more chicken.

"Bandawe says he saw prisoners in irons and chains. Europeans used whips made of hippo hides on their domestic servants and labourers."

Ouma pointed a finger at Dominee. "Stop lecturing to us. Have you ever seen us whip our servants or labourers? We may not come to church but we're good Christians."

"Ouma, I'm just telling you what I read in the paper," said Dominee frowning at Adam who was sucking on chicken bones.

"Ja, and African labourers are well off under the Labour Tenancy Act with two and a half acres of land, some stock, farm equipment so they can earn a little money," said Ouma turning to

Adam. "What do you think Adam?"

He shrugged and Ouma muttered under her breath. "Have you nothing to say?"

Tania piped up. "Would be better if they could own their own farms though, don't you think?"

The sarcasm in her daughter's voice was obvious to Miriam, and the conversation was beginning to make her feel tense. But at least Tania had got Adam's attention.

Still eating he replied. "They can own land in their own Reserves."

Ouma was the only one to smile at his contribution. "We're very generous giving land to the African, aren't we Adam?"

"Ouma, how can you say such a thing? Europeans own most of the land and just think how many Africans live on this continent." Tania's voice was barely above a whisper.

"Where do these ideas of yours come from? Miriam, I told you Tania should have gone to our local Afrikaans school not that liberal English school."

Miriam threw a warning look at Tania who shrugged and pulled a face. Miriam remained silent. Ouma wore blinkers like a horse unable to accept views opposed to her own. What worried her more was Tania being very vocal about her opinions that differed from most of their community.

Changing the subject Miriam turned to Adam. "Adam, are you working on your pa's farm?"

"Yes, but it doesn't belong to Pa. He's the farm manager but talks as if the farm belongs to him."

Miriam was silent. She was feeling tense today knowing that she was walking a tightrope keeping the relationship with Hendrik secret. She had a feeling that Dominee had his suspicions. She would have to be careful, all too aware of the tight-knit community in which they lived. She didn't have much to do with them but Ouma did and she had to think about Tania. Her excuse was that she had too much to do on the farm and didn't have time for community involvement.

Dominee turned a page in the newspaper and began reading.

"Chelembwe rebelled against the Europeans in Nyasaland, and murdered them. Members of his tribe were caught and hanged."

Ouma covered her ears with her hands. "Why am I still alive to hear such terrible things? I should be dead and resting in peace already."

There was silence at the table broken by Cook chasing one of the hens through the house. Nervous laughter followed her as she snatched the hen, swearing under her breath lest Ouma hear.

It was 1916. Miriam busied herself in the books. They were not doing much business but anything was better than looking at Ouma's morose face. She was tired of Ouma talking about dying. There was food to eat and she had a warm clean bed to sleep in, but she could tell Ouma was not herself. She kept talking about dreams upsetting her. Well she couldn't order happy dreams for Ouma. One morning at breakfast Ouma didn't eat a thing.

"What's wrong, are you feeling ill?" Miriam asked anxious to get away to the office.

"I heard my name called in a dream, Miriam. It was an angel singing my name and it sounded beautiful, and then she said it was 'time'. What do you think the angel meant? Do you think it's my time to die?"

Miriam sighed. She didn't have "time" for this now. "Ouma, perhaps you have an angel watching over you. Maybe, she means it's time you get involved again in the farm. It's not good for you to just give up because there's a war going on." She struggled to keep a serious face when she saw Ouma looking suspiciously at her.

Then Ouma nodded, "Maybe you're right."

"You know Ouma, you don't believe a woman can run a farm successfully. Well, I heard that a woman has planted an apple orchard. She's managing a farm on her own." She waited for Ouma's reply.

Ouma tapped on the table and took her time before replying.

"We'll wait and see if she's successful, shall we?"

"I heard she planted Versveld and Reineete de Canada trees and called the apples Ohenimuri. If she can do it, why can't we?"

"Where does she get the trees from?"

"From Rhodes Fruit Farms."

"Well, what are you waiting for? Write to them," said Ouma with a toothless smile.

"Ouma, you've forgotten your false teeth again. Do you want me to fetch them?"

"Ag, could be worse. Could've forgotten to put my panties on. I'll get them myself. More important you write to this fruit farm."

" But, Britain has prohibited import of fresh fruit because they need cargo space for the war."

"Wars don't last forever and we can sell locally," retorted Ouma, as she dunked a rusk in her tea. Without her teeth, she made a slurping sound as she sucked the rusk, irritating Miriam. To blot out the noise Miriam picked up the newspaper. She couldn't bear to think of the suffering the war was causing. She read on quietly thinking how to get Ouma to help on the farm. Maybe Ouma could do a little baking which she said she had always enjoyed, not that Miriam could ever remember seeing her bake. It would have to be with Cook's agreement of course.

Miriam felt physically ill reading about all the animals that had died in the war, and read that an Australian vet committed suicide he was so distressed. She put the paper down unable to read further and when she entered the kitchen she found Cook in a state.

"Miss Miriam, I've just taken some food to one of our labourers. He's returned ill from the fighting. He looks like a skeleton Miss Miriam. He carried forty pound food parcels on his head for the troops and he went hungry. Surely that's not right. He was a carrier and not allowed a gun."

"I know Cook but their contribution hasn't gone unnoticed." She didn't mention the number of deaths. "Have you had any news about your man Cook?"

"No, Miss Miriam. I don't know if he's alive or dead. He's all I've got. I have no children to support me," said Cook in a choked voice.

"Sit down Cook. I want you to know you can live on the farm as long as you wish. You're part of our family and besides without you Ouma would pick a fight with me."

Cook smiled through her tears and Thembeki stood at the kitchen door, tears rolling down her cheeks. Cook took one look at her. "What are you crying about?" blew her nose and got up to stir the soup.

Miriam winked at Thembeki who donned an apron and began to knead the dough.

~ ~ ~

Dominee came by with some koeksisters one Sunday morning after church. "Miriam, I brought these for Ouma, a gift from the women in my church. I know she loves them. How is she today?"

"Why don't you give them to Ouma yourself. She hardly eats anything these days. She's in bed today. Dominee, how am I going to manage on the farm with the call to arms?"

"I can help you Mama," said Tania.

Dominee patted Tania's hand. "I'm sure you're a help to your mama. You know what Grogan said – women are indispensable if you want anything done well."

Tania laughed. "Well Papa, tell this Grogan from me that women are always the ones to get things done."

"See Dominee, how the new generation think," said Miriam. "You can also tell Grogan if he dispenses with my workforce, that will only leave us women to get all the work done."

"I'll go and see Ouma now if you don't mind?"

Miriam smiled at his haste to get away from them and winked at Tania.

♣ ♣ ♣

"So, tell me Dominee, why the troubled look?" Ouma sat up in bed and fluffed up her pillows.

"War Ouma, but we're fortunate to have Botha and Smuts as leaders. Union was such an achievement in 1910 and shows our loyalty to the Crown. Six years later and look at the tension between us Afrikaners. Hertzog is a fanatic and extremist with his cry, 'Africa for the Afrikaner.'"

"Tell me Dominee, what's wrong with that. If I were a man, I'd go and fight with Hertzog."

"Ouma, he's excluding black Africans. He's a dangerous man."

"That's your view, not mine Dominee. What happened to De la Rey? You know the General whom Dirk fought under."

"He joined Hertzog and was shot at a police roadblock in Johannesburg."

"Such a brave man. He was a hero Dominee."

"Ja Ouma, but Smuts has a point when he says that a greater South Africa can only be created alongside the British Empire."

"Won't you have a koeksister with your tea, Ouma?" He pushed the plate towards her.

Ouma dunked one in her tea and took a bite. "Did you make these Dominee? They're hard as blerrie leather. Where did you get these?"

Dominee swallowed. "The women in my church brought them for you Ouma."

Ouma put the koeksister down. "Dominee, those women you speak of, who used to be my friends, no longer visit me. You expect me to believe you? Ever since Miriam took up with Hendrik, I haven't seen them for dust. So, what do you have to say?"

Ouma waited. "Think I didn't know about Miriam and Hendrik Dominee? First time you've been lost for words. I'm tired. Come and talk to me tomorrow, and don't bring stale koeksisters with you, hear?" She closed her eyes.

Dominee shrugged, got up and left.

♣ ♣ ♣

It was the summer of 1918 and Dominee came running up the

front steps. He waved the paper at Ouma and Miriam sitting on the stoep. "The war is over. Look what the paper says," and read on out of breath. "The Germans have surrendered," and lowered his voice. "About ninety-five thousand carriers recruited by the British have died."

Miriam thought of Cook's husband. "Dominee please don't say anything to Cook."

He shook his head. "No, of course I won't."

"I think we need something stronger than tea," and went to get some wine. She filled their glasses and raised hers. "We must drink to the future. If only we didn't have an outbreak of Spanish flu. Cook says it's God punishing us for this war." Her thoughts turned to Hendrik. There still was no word from him, and she thought of going to visit his wife. Maybe she had heard from him? But couldn't bring herself to do so. Her feelings for Hendrik might be written all over her face. She'd never heard him talk about his wife or children. How happy could he be at home if he found solace in her bed? She trembled fearing he wouldn't make it back to her.

Miriam was relieved that Ouma seemed to be back to her old self again, and one good thing had come out of Ouma's dreams, she now believed an angel watched over her.

"Those African women whose husbands returned from war, wear smiles on their faces. Others weren't so fortunate," said Dominee. "We wouldn't have won the war without the carriers you know."

"Did you hear Dominee, there's a campaign for racial segregation. The South African National Native's Council have written to King George V asking him to rid them of oppression and give them voting rights," Miriam said with one eye on her knitting.

"Sounds ominous to me," said Adam sitting in the background.

Miriam heard Ouma grunt appreciatively.

"Don't you think the African has rights?" Tania turned on Adam waving a newspaper in his face.

Miriam diverted the conversation quickly. "Cook's husband hasn't returned yet Dominee and she's given up hope."

"I know Miriam. They gave their lives to this country. Bishop Willis from Uganda said that the 'African and European in Africa need one another,' and if the 'African's progress is held up there'll be a terrible retribution.'"

Miriam shivered as if this were an omen. Dominee was always quoting from the newspaper or some source or other. She drew her shawl around her shoulders and felt relief that the war was finally over. Now she could get back to building up the farm again. If only Hendrik were safely in her arms. Looking up she saw a man striding up the long path towards the farm house. She dropped the knitting and began to run, tripping over her long skirt. Hendrik helped her up, gathering her in his arms as she laughed and cried.

Her words came out in a rush, "I was so afraid for you Hendrik. You're home now thank God."

He kissed her gently and disengaged himself, "Miriam, I'm very tired. I came straight here to see you."

Miriam took his hand, "Will you come by tonight? We've been apart for such a long time, and I've missed you so much Hendrik."

"I can't Miriam. I must spend some time with my family. I'll be back at work tomorrow. I'd better go now."

Miriam reluctantly let go of his hand and watched him as he walked slowly back down the avenue. He turned round to wave and she waved back with a heavy heart. Tomorrow seemed a long time away.

Ouma spluttered. "Talk to Miriam, Dominee. This has to stop."

Tania took Adam by the hand and they went indoors. Dominee rose up from his chair. "Ouma, it's not my place to interfere."

"Nonsense, you're close to Miriam. You talk to her, she'll listen to you. People are talking Dominee." She gripped the chair, "I tell you it's a scandal. Hendrik has a wife and family."

"Ouma, don't upset yourself so." Dominee called out, "Thembeki, come take Ouma to her room, she needs to rest."

Ouma stumbled as she tried to stand and Dominee helped her up. Thembeki came running, and took Ouma's hand whilst Dominee marched off without a backward glance shaking his head and mumbling under his breath.

The following morning Miriam couldn't wait to get to the office and missed breakfast. Searching for keys to open the office door she looked up and saw Anika striding towards her. She hurriedly opened the door and stepped inside and was about to close the door when Anika shoved it open.

"I need to talk to you." Anika slammed the door shut pointing her finger in Miriam's face. "You leave my husband alone, do you understand me?"

Miriam gripped the arm of the chair. "What are you talking about?"

Anika's eyes were narrow slits and her voice was high pitched. "Hendrik's a good man and you're leading him astray. He's my husband not yours."

"I don't know what you're talking about. Hendrik works for me and he has to work late sometimes. It's all part of his job."

Anika looked round the office. "I know he doesn't work late into the night in this office. You see, I've come looking for my husband when he said he'd be working late, and he wasn't here. He made up a story he'd been drinking, but there was no liquor on his breath. I'm not stupid. He's been in your bed. A woman can tell. I know you're lying. He's mine and you leave him alone."

Miriam took a deep breath, "I never meant to come between you and your husband. It just happened."

"Is that all you can say? It just happened. What happened? Oh, don't tell me, I'd rather not know. You keep away from my Hendrik do you understand me?" She walked out slamming the door behind her.

Miriam slumped in the chair feeling shaky. Hendrik must have been having a hard time at home but hadn't breathed a word to her. She would keep Anika's tirade to herself.

~ ~ ~

The 1920s began with celebrations when Adam approached Miriam one evening. She looked up noticing Tania prodding Adam.

Adam's voice shook a little. "Miriam, can I speak to you for a moment?"

"Yes of course. For goodness' sake sit down, you're making me nervous." Out of the corner of her eye she saw Ouma grinning.

"I'd like to ask your permission to marry Tania." Adam slipped his hand into Tania's.

"Thank goodness, thought I'd have to end up asking," giggled Tania whilst Ouma laughed.

"Well Mama, what do you say?" said Tania.

Miriam got up and hugged them. "I'm delighted for you both. Tania's over to you now Adam."

"What's that supposed to mean?" said Tania.

"It was a joke Tania, that's all." Miriam sighed. She always seemed to say the wrong thing.

"Whatever you say about me won't scare him Mama. We'd like a small wedding and for Papa to marry us of course."

"You'd better ask Dominee, and we'll have the wedding at home. Adam, I've been thinking. Would you like to work alongside Hendrik as his Assistant?"

"I'd love to work on your farm," said Adam shaking Miriam's hand.

"Good, that's settled. And, would you like to move in after you're married?" Miriam looked from Adam to Tania who were both all smiles.

Tania spoke for them both, "We'd love that, wouldn't we Adam?"

Adam nodded and Tania kissed Ouma who shook Adam's hand and said, "About time you two."

"Now you'd better go and tell Thembeki and Cook." Miriam heard squeals of delight coming from the kitchen.

Adam's father Jan was invited to Sunday lunch, and Thembeki and Cook went to town with preparations.

Jan took Miriam's hand in his. "Adam's a good boy and is a hard worker. He told me he'll be living on your farm when they get married."

Miriam withdrew her hand. "Yes, it'll be more convenient for Adam and Tania to live here especially as Adam will be working with me."

Tania and Adam's marriage was a quiet affair and brought back the past for Miriam. It was a hot summer's night when Miriam stirred in her sleep. Half-awake she threw off the bedcovers. Rubbing her eyes she recalled her dream. She was in Joseph's arms but he was looking over his shoulder at Hannah. Always, Hannah stood in the background. Joseph was tied to Hannah just as Hendrik was tied to his wife, Anika. The name Anika never passed her lips. She didn't want to think about her. Anika always appeared to loom over Hendrik in her dreams. It felt like an omen especially as he seemed more distant lately. He still came to her at night but at greater intervals and never stayed late into the night. She was afraid to ask any questions especially after Anika's outburst. She had no intention of telling him about it.

In the morning over breakfast Miriam found herself talking about her dream. "Strange, I dreamed about Joseph and his father being photographed. It happened such a long time ago, Ouma." She shivered.

"Who is Joseph?" Ouma no longer laughed at dreams.

"I grew up with Joseph, and our families travelled from Poland together." Miriam looked away remembering the pain. "Joseph met Hannah on the ship and disembarked with her in England. We carried on alone to South Africa." It still hurt to talk about the past. A silence followed whilst Miriam thought about the wooden heart that she would often take out of her drawer and think about Joseph. If only she hadn't been so innocent and naïve .

Ouma frowned. "It's fate, just accept it. Like now, I feel my time is drawing near and the angels are talking to me. But, don't you tell Dominee I talk about angels." Ouma wagged a finger at her.

"Ouma," Miriam began. She could hardly contain her excitement. A letter had been delivered that morning. It was from England. Her hands shook as she'd opened the letter. After reading the contents it had taken her a while to come down to earth.

"Ja, what is it? I've had enough talk of dreams for one day."

"I've received a letter from Joseph. He's written to say he'd like to bring his family to see South Africa one day and hopes to visit our farm. He says it may be some time still before work allows him to do so," she added touching the letter in her pocket and feeling sixteen again. She could only think that Joseph hadn't forgotten her.

"Does Hendrik know about this man?"

Miriam frowned. "Ouma, what does it have to do with Hendrik? Joseph is an old friend and anyway who knows when they might be coming to visit."

"Has Dominee had a word with you about Hendrik?"

Miriam knew what was coming. "Why should he?" She turned to go scraping the chair as she got up.

"He's a married man and people are talking. The community will shun us."

"That's my business so let them shun us," and she stormed out of the room. But, anxiety was getting to her. It was the changes in Hendrik's behaviour that made her uneasy. Most days he would leave work early and rarely came to her at night. She was afraid to ask questions grateful for the times he did come to her, but he was always in a hurry to get home. She missed lying in his arms and talking long into the night.

Ouma let out a heavy sigh and got up slowly. Her hands trembled as she lent on her walking stick. Slowly she made her way to the stoep struggling a little to see where she was going.

Tania surprised Ouma with a hug. "I'm going for a swim in the river with Adam. It's wonderful to feel weightless in the water with my bump Ouma. Do you want to come with us?"

Ouma smiled. "Can Adam carry an old woman so far? Has your ma told you her friend Joseph may be coming to visit?"

"Who is Joseph?" asked Tania.

"Better ask your ma," said Ouma.

"Mama has more time to talk to you than me," said Tania and walked off waving to Dominee.

Ouma mumbled, "Why don't those blerrie angels help when I need them," and felt hands reach out to steady her.

"You should come quicker next time. What's the use of being an angel if you're not there the instant I need you? Oh, it's you."

"Never thought I'd qualify as an angel in your eyes," said Dominee with a smile, taking Ouma by the hand. "Where do you want to go?"

"Inside. It's too blerrie hot sitting here." Together they walked slowly indoors. "None of my friends visit me anymore Dominee. Will you say a prayer in church and forgive Miriam and Hendrik. Maybe they'll come and see me then."

He squeezed Ouma's hand. "I can't forgive them. Hendrik's wife must forgive them."

Ouma sighed. "Why wasn't I told we're going into apple farming?"

"Ouma, Miriam talked about moving into apple farming some time ago. Have you forgotten?"

"I don't remember so well these days. It's hard to remember everything that happens around the farm," she looked up at him through tears.

Dominee patted her hand and helped her sit down. Her head dropped forward and he left her sleeping in the chair.

Miriam returning from the office caught Thembeki taking Ouma a cup of tea. "I'll take it to her Thembeki."

"Miss Miriam, Ouma hasn't been herself lately. Shouldn't she see a doctor?"

"There's nothing a doctor can do to help her. She's getting old

Thembeki."

She found Ouma clutching a cushion. "What are you doing with that cushion. It belongs in your bedroom."

"No, it doesn't. I'm tidying up." A little bewildered, she put the cushion down. "I've been thinking. What happened to that lovely family your mama was friendly with in Cape Town?"

Miriam frowned. The things Ouma remembered she wished she wouldn't. "We lost touch. It was too far for them to visit us on the farm."

"Hmm, such a pity. They had a young son your age. Is he married yet? Your mama said something about a letter from David meant for you that she lost?"

"Ouma, you're like one of our matchmakers from the Schtetl. David was going to study medicine the last I heard, and Mama never mentioned anything to me about a letter from him." Miriam felt her patience was being tried. Ouma was rambling on and she never knew whether it was stories she was making up in her head. Ouma, I have everything I want right here."

Ouma muttered. "Well, what about Piet then?"

"You're an obstinate old woman. You don't listen to me."

"Then end up like me."

"I'd be happy to end up like you, living on this farm with my grandchild."

"Is Tania going to have a baby?" Ouma's eyes lit up then she frowned, "why didn't she tell me?"

"She did Ouma. You must have forgotten. She's quite far gone already. Haven't you noticed?"

"Well, she was always well covered." She frowned. "She talked about a bump not a baby," picking up the cushion and clutching it to her chest.

"I must get back to work Ouma. I'll ask Tania to take you for a short walk. It'll do you good to get some fresh air."

Miriam kissed Ouma. "You're spending too much time on your own these days."

"Whose fault is that?" Muttering to herself, "if you spent more time with your daughter maybe you'd get on better," and watched Miriam walk off to the office.

It was early in the morning when Miriam heard Tania calling her. She knew instantly it was time and quickly put on a dressing gown.

"Mama, my waters have broken and I'm having contractions. Please stay with me."

"I won't leave you Tania. Adam, go call the doctor. Don't just stand there – move for goodness' sake unless you want to deliver the baby yourself."

Miriam rubbed Tania's back and made her comfortable. She kept walking to the window but there was no sign of the doctor.

"Mama, the contractions are coming quicker. Why isn't the doctor here yet?"

"He'll be here soon," and shouted, "Adam, did you call the doctor?"

Adam took the stairs two at a time. "He's on his way."

"Get out of here Adam," screamed Tania.

Miriam heard the doorbell and peered round the door. "Don't stand there Adam. That must be the doctor, go show him up now. Oh dear, men are so helpless at these times."

"Hope that doesn't include me," said Doctor Retief taking the stairs two at a time and closing the door on Adam. "I'm in the nick of time I see. Baby's in a hurry to be born Tania."

Miriam felt a sense of joy that Tania wanted her to be present at the birth.

"Another push Tania. I can see the baby's head," said the doctor. "Well done, my dear you have a son."

"He's beautiful," exclaimed Miriam kissing Tania and caressing the soft hair on the baby's head. "I'll go get Adam for you."

Adam was puffing on his pipe and walking up and down the corridor.

Miriam was all smiles. "You have a son Adam. You can go in now. But first put that pipe out. I'll let everyone know the good news." She took the stairs slowly touching Joseph's letter in her pocket. It was crumpled from having read it so often, but still in one piece. Every time she read his letter it made her think of what might have been.

Ivy Cottage
Amersham
England

My Dear Miriam,

It has taken me a long time to put words to paper. I am a man of few words so Hannah tells me. It may be true. I relied on my mama to keep in touch with you and your family. Sadly, Mama and Papa have long since passed away as has Sarah. I miss my family. My Grandmother was someone I could confide in although less so as a young man. She was a wise old lady and knew I would need to look after the family. My papa would not have been able to support us in a different environment to the one in which he had grown up. Life was hard enough for him and he struggled to make a living and pay for my education.

Miriam, I have an enduring memory of the last time I saw you when we disembarked in England. I was young and my family's future weighed heavily on my shoulders. I often wonder how my future would have turned out had I continued on to South Africa. I have regrets but imagine that is the same for many of us not so? We're all faced with challenges in life. I was so sorry to hear about your dear Papa. When I'm sitting by the fire images of our youth spring to mind. Do you remember me teaching you to read and write? I think of you often and wonder whether you still have the little wooden heart I gave you? It was all I could give you. I was afraid of what was to come when we left our lives in the Schtetl.

I've made a life with Hannah. We live in a large rambling house that seems very quiet and lonely without my son, Mark. He is studying medicine and returns home during his holidays. Hannah keeps herself busy with charity work and we lead a quiet life.

The business has enabled me to be able to consider the prospect of travelling. Hannah has agreed after much persuasion to visit South Africa. I would love to see you and your family and we'll certainly have a lot of reminiscing to do. It may be some time, however, before I can think of taking time off from the business. When I'm able to do so I will get in touch hopefully in the not too distant future.

Your old friend,

Joseph

~ ~ ~

A seed hidden in the heart of an apple is an orchard invisible, 1925

The family huddled round the fireplace whilst Daniel now five years old sat quietly looking at a picture book. Winter was cold in the Palmiet Valley, a climate ideal for growing apples. Miriam placed another log on the fire and took her time gathering her thoughts together. "I've been talking to our neighbour and he said we can buy apples trees from him." Excited about the future she waited for Hendrik's response.

Hendrik stood with legs astride. "We know nothing about fruit farming. Besides, it'll be an expensive exercise."

She hadn't expected him to be negative, and gave him a questioning look.

Adam raised his glass of wine to Miriam. "Wonderful idea. It's about time we experiment. Why don't you sit down Hendrik?"

Hendrik remained standing with his head held high. Miriam disappointed with his reaction turned to Adam. "Will you contact Elgin Co-operative Fruit Growers for me? They'll give us the information we need."

"We can thank Jan van Riebeeck who brought the first sweet apple seedlings to the Cape in 1652," said Dominee.

"Papa, how do you know it was van Riebeeck?" Tania inclined

her head towards him.

"Read about it," said Dominee.

"You're a walking encyclopaedia Papa," she laughed.

"I suppose they stem from Adam and Eve's day?" said Hendrik inclining his head towards Dominee.

Miriam frowned at the sarcasm in Hendrik's tone of voice. Something had changed between them. She knew she was hanging on by a thread but she wasn't prepared to give him up.

Dominee ignored Hendrik, took another sip of wine, and continued unabated. "Ten million years ago an early form of the apple, size of a cherry, was traced to the mountain ranges of Inner and Central Asia. Seeds were distributed by birds and animals and today we have the apple."

"Do you know when the first apple trees were grown?" Tania asked.

"Think back about ten thousand years when humans changed from hunter, fisher-gatherer people to a more settled existence. They planted crops and stored food. In Babylon, as much as three thousand eight hundred years ago, they grafted fruit trees, and their knowledge spread through wars and conquest."

"How interesting," said Hendrik looking at his watch.

Dominee was in full flow now. "Today, grafting has enabled individual cultivar trees to be preserved through cloning."

Hendrik swung round to face Dominee. "Since you know everything, you can save us having to ask for information."

"Hendrik!" exclaimed Miriam. "What's the matter with you? Dominee doesn't deserve to be spoken to like that."

Hendrik put his glass down and made for the door. "I'm going home. Miriam, as your manager, you should've spoken to me first about buying apple trees from Jan."

Miriam winced when the door banged shut behind him. "I'll go talk to him."

"Ag, just leave him. He'll come around when he sees a profit," said Ouma.

Miriam ignored Ouma and rushed out. "Hendrik, wait a minute please."

He didn't look round and Miriam ran to catch up with him. She hadn't wanted to confront him but she had no choice.

"Hendrik, please don't speak to me like that in front of my family."

Hendrik continued walking. "I'll speak my mind wherever I may be, especially when you don't tell me about plans for the farm. I would have thought you'd consult me first."

"Look at me Hendrik. I wanted to discuss it with the family. For goodness' sake I asked you to be present, and you're not always present these days."

Hendrik stopped dead. "What's that supposed to mean?"

"When I'm with you it doesn't feel the same. It's as if you're somewhere else." She reached for his hand but he walked off leaving her to catch up with him.

"Hendrik, what is wrong?"

He shrugged. "I must get home. I don't have time to talk right now. I'll see you tomorrow."

Miriam stood staring after him. Downcast she walked back not knowing what to think.

The family had gone to bed except for Dominee and Adam who were having a drink in the front room.

Adam drink in hand was watching through the window. When he saw Miriam return he closed the curtains quickly and went to open the front door. "Miriam, I'll speak to Elgin Fruit Growers. I want you to know I'm behind you all the way."

Miriam merely nodded with her mind in turmoil thinking about Hendrik.

"I'd better be going. Goodnight." Dominee put his glass down and Miriam saw him out.

Miriam wondered what Hendrik saw when he looked at her now? Slowly age was creeping up on her. A few grey hairs and wrinkles. Is that what he saw? She went up to bed. The sheets were cold and she couldn't get warm. She tried not to think about him and visualized planting apple trees. Eventually she felt herself lulled to sleep with sounds of the wind rustling the branches outside her window.

She woke the next morning feeling more optimistic and certain apple production was their future. More and more farmers were turning their hand to fruit farming. She had to move with the times or be left behind. She hired more labourers as row upon row of apple trees were planted with potatoes and onions in the shade of the trees. A furrow was built to irrigate the land. They used wood stave pipes, and she watched Adam working side by side with the labourers. She saw his determination to learn first hand about all aspects of apple growing. He got up early in the mornings to collect kraal manure and fertiliser and dig it in alongside the labourers. Together they inspected the apple trees almost daily. Miriam asked jokingly. "How are your babies doing?"

"Growing beautifully," Adam answered in a serious tone and laughed when Miriam described Daniel as "her little farmer".

Daniel grew up almost unnoticed by his father whose attention was focused on the orchards. He tried to get the attention of his father and got up especially early in the mornings to join him and Michael who assisted Adam on their rounds of the orchards. At first he enjoyed himself. He watched his father and Michael examine the trees for any disease. Heard his father sigh with relief when all was found to be well. He liked Michael, who lifted him onto his shoulders so he could see to the end of the orchard. This lasted only until Michael couldn't lift him anymore.

"You're growing too fast. Quicker than these trees. You're almost up to my shoulder now," said Michael smoking a pipe. Daniel tried the pipe once when Michael wasn't looking, coughing and spitting out tobacco. He listened to his father and Michael talking.

"You found a woman yet Michael?" Adam winked at Daniel.

"No Master Adam."

"Well, what about Cook?"

"She'd flatten me. I couldn't risk it."

They laughed and Adam clapped him on the back. Daniel joined in imagining what Michael might look like flattened.

Slowly year by year the trees grew. "We mustn't strain these trees. Another year and they'll bear quality fruit for us," said Adam.

"Four years since planting, Master Adam."

"Patience Michael."

One Saturday morning Adam brought a hip flask with him. "Come on. Have a little shnaps with me."

"So early in the morning, Master Adam."

"Why not?" said Adam. "Ever had woman trouble Michael?" pouring whiskey into two tin cups. "This stuff anaesthetizes all troubles even though it burns my throat."

Daniel watched as the men imbibed and his father sank back against an old gnarled apple tree. He would have liked to try whiskey but wasn't offered any.

"This tree is the baby of the orchard," said Adam drinking from the bottle.

Michael turned away to spit out tobacco, and noticed Daniel was nowhere to be seen. "Daniel?" he called out and started striding towards the dam. Something caught his eye. A movement on the ground ahead of him. Daniel was kneeling with a stick in his hand and Michael followed his gaze. There in front of the boy was a puff-adder. He put his finger to his lips when Daniel looked up. The large African viper had inflated the upper part of its body and was ready to strike. Daniel watched its tongue going in and out, unable to move. Michael seized the moment. Picked up a stone and threw it to the side of the snake to distract it. Grabbing Daniel they ran. Breathing heavily he panted. "Don't you ever play with puff-adders again, they're poisonous. It's time you learned about snakes. Remember, they're more frightened of you," but he was shaking as they walked towards the farmhouse leaving Adam to sleep off his schnaps.

♣ ♣ ♣

Miriam heard the row between Adam and Tania that night, thick though the walls were in the homestead. It was the effect on Daniel that worried her most. Adam's drinking had become a problem but she held back from interfering in their marriage. She felt guilty having been absorbed in making ends meet, she hadn't had the energy to spend more time with Tania as she was growing up. A wall of silence had built up between them but she still tried though the solution evaded her.

She took her time over breakfast waiting for Adam to go and turned to Tania. "I couldn't help but hear you and Adam row last night. I don't want you to think I'm interfering, but would it help if you got more involved in the farm?" Miriam waited and tensed when Tania pushed her plate away and stood up.

"I don't think you're the person to go to for advice about relationships, and don't interfere in mine." Tania turned her back on her mama and walked out.

Miriam felt heartsore. This was the price she was paying for devoting all her time to the farm.

It was four years since the planting of the first apple trees, and when August came around there were buds on the trees. In September, Miriam stood with Adam admiring the blossoms on the apple trees. She beamed at him. "Come on, let's see how our beauties are doing." They walked side by side down the rows.

"We've planted several varieties and only time will tell which will do best," said Adam examining their handiwork carefully.

Miriam could smell whiskey on his breath but she knew Michael was always around to see that tasks got done.

"I must get to the office now Adam. I'll see you later." Her stomach felt in knots these days not knowing where she stood with Hendrik and afraid to confront him.

She felt a sense of relief to see him at his desk. He stood up as she entered.

"Miriam, I'm leaving."

"Leaving? What do you mean?" She sat down heavily.

"I have to go. You know why."

"I need you Hendrik," and hated the desperation and pleading in her voice.

"No, you don't."

To Miriam his voice sounded devoid of emotion. "But Hendrik, you manage this farm, you have a good job. Do you need more pay?"

"Since when do I manage this farm anymore. Adam is your right hand man these days. Don't think I haven't noticed you giving him more responsibility."

"I know you two don't get on very well but we can sort that out."

"Miriam, you can be naïve sometimes. I can't work with the man, never mind get on with him. He's an inebriated … it can't be easily sorted. My mind's made up. I'm going."

"What about us?" Miriam looked at Hendrik blinking away tears.

"I have to think of my family. I can't leave my family and I never promised you I would."

Miriam couldn't stop the tears. She reached out to take his hand. He took a step back. "I'm leaving today." His voice faltered. "I start my new job tomorrow."

The shock made her feel dazed. She couldn't find the words to make him change his mind. She watched him go without a backward glance, gripped the chair as she got up, and walked blindly out of the office, her mind in turmoil. She should have been prepared but knew she'd ignored all the warning signs. She took a detour to Dirk's grave where she sat with her head bowed. How was she to carry on alone?

"Grandma, I've been looking for you. It's suppertime. Is something wrong?" asked Daniel.

"Nothing you need worry about. Give me a moment." She had to pull herself together. Daniel helped her up and she hugged him. Together they walked towards the farmhouse. Miriam tried to focus her mind on her grandson, "Are you looking forward to boarding school Daniel?"

He hesitated before answering. "I don't know Grandma."

She took his hand. "You'll make new friends and school holidays will come around before you know it. What's in your hand?"

He handed her a letter. "It's for you. Pa says it's from England."

Miriam recognised the handwriting. "I'll join you at supper in a moment," and went straight up to her bedroom closing the door. It was a letter from Joseph announcing the date of their arrival. They were planning to visit in February when apples would be ready for picking. How strange that Joseph should come back into her life when she was feeling at her most vulnerable. She placed the letter in her pocket. She'd almost given up on Joseph visiting. He'd got her hopes up and then not written again until now with an actual date. Tania and Adam appeared not to notice her silence at the supper table for which she was grateful as she struggled to eat. She was still in shock. She never expected Hendrik to leave.

Miriam knew she'd have to tell them. It was better to get it over with and struggled to find the right words, "Hendrik is leaving …" And taking a deep breath her next words came out in a whisper, "He has a new job."

Tania got up and put her arms around her ma. "I'm so sorry Ma."

Adam sat up and said, "Perhaps it's for the best Ma."

"I think I'll go to bed now," and left not wanting either of them to see her tears.

Tania took Ouma supper in bed. "The orchard is looking beautiful Ouma, and the apples have a funny name; O'Heni Muri and Golden Delicious. Mama has planted chives, perstimmons and nasturtiums around the trees, and the chickens have free run of the orchards."

"What are chickens doing running around an orchard?" Ouma peered at the food on her plate.

"They eat the insects, saw-fly and codling moth."

"Well, this food looks like it'll be good for those insects. You tell Cook I'm not eating this rubbish. What is it?"

"It's bobotie Ouma, your favourite, and I wouldn't risk telling Cook what you've just said. I value my life!" Tania laughed.

Ouma tasted the mince and tucked in. "I'll have to teach Cook how to make bobotie. So, when did you say these trees were planted?"

Tania replied gently. "In August and September, four years ago Ouma, don't you remember me telling you? They're pruned in winter, and we'll be ready to pick the apples soon in February."

"No, I don't remember because you didn't tell me," said Ouma with a mouth full of food.

"I'll bring you the first apple of the season to taste," Tania added, wiping food off Ouma's bed jacket.

When Ouma was finished and made comfortable in bed, Tania took the tray and finished the leftovers before going into Cook's kitchen, passing her mama going to bed.

"Couldn't Ouma manage to eat it all?" asked Miriam.

"Ouma said it was rubbish. Says she's going to teach Cook how to make bobotie."

Miriam managed a smile. "Tania, I know you're worried about sending Daniel to boarding school, but it'll be good for him. He's tougher than you think." Tania didn't answer. Miriam hesitated and the words rushed out. "I haven't had time to look at improvements for our labourers. Could you look into it for me?"

Tania shrugged. "If you make time to talk to me first about the details," and paused. "I suppose I could fit it in with pottery," and without another word she continued down the stairs.

Miriam stood watching Tania at a loss for words. It felt more like a cement barrier between them.

JOSEPH'S VISIT, 1930s

The sun was streaming in through the windows. The apples were harvested, and it looked like they had a good crop. Miriam was thinking of Joseph due to arrive at the farm today and she was all jittery.

"Tania, won't you help me choose a dress?"

"What's the matter with you Mama? Why do you need my help?"

Miriam didn't reply and ran her hand over the dresses thrown onto the bed. "I don't know what to wear. They're either too tight or not 'right for the occasion'."

Tania picked up a floral patterned dress. "This might take ten years off you."

Miriam felt irritated by the remark. "Oh, I don't know."

Tania threw her hands up in the air. "For goodness' sake, what's all the palaver about? I'll leave you to decide as you don't want to listen to my advice."

Miriam picked out a white blouse and tucked it into a three quarter length skirt. She stood a while looking in the mirror thinking back to the velvet dress she'd worn for Joseph when she was sixteen. Her hair was greying but she was still slim. She put lipstick on and put all the clothes back in the cupboard. Holding on to the banister to steady herself she made her way downstairs. Ouma was finishing breakfast but Miriam couldn't eat and sat sipping a cup of tea.

Ouma pointed a finger at her. "It's your fault Hendrik left us. He was an experienced manager and Dirk's right hand."

Miriam was tense and this was the last thing she felt like talking about. "I know you're upset Ouma, but you have to accept that people move on." She could never admit that she was having a hard time with Hendrik gone.

"People move on only when they have good reason to do so, and I know what his was. Now who will run this farm?"

"Ouma, you surprise me. I've been running this farm since Dirk's death, and we couldn't ask for a better manager than Adam."

Ouma looked at Adam who was helping himself to eggs and bacon. "I knew all along your affair would lead to this. I trusted in the man. I don't feel like eating anymore. Thembeki, help me up. I want to go and sit on the stoep."

Miriam waited till Ouma left the room and turned to Adam. "Ouma's upset with me not you, Adam."

Adam shrugged. "It's nothing to do with me Miriam," and continued to tuck into his food.

Miriam caught Tania staring at her low cut blouse. She tugged at it as it was slightly too tight and walked past her daughter and out to the stoep. Shortly afterwards a chug, chug, chug could be heard. A Ford car was coming down the drive. The car door opened and a tall, grey haired man climbed out. Joseph was unmistakeable and she drew in her breath. He made an imposing figure. Then she saw Hannah, slim and beautifully dressed, in what she supposed to be the latest fashion. She was being helped out of the car by a young man. To Miriam he looked like a younger version of his father. She stumbled as she made her way towards the car.

"You haven't changed," said Joseph wrapping his arms around Miriam.

He released her when Hannah exclaimed. "We've come a long way to see your country."

Miriam kissed Hannah on the cheek and shook hands with Mark. "It's so wonderful to see you all," never taking her eyes off Joseph. The family are waiting to meet you," and led Joseph by the hand with Hannah and Mark following.

Ouma squinted up at Joseph through thick glasses that kept sliding down her nose. He shook hands with everyone and introduced Hannah and Mark.

"Are you married young man?"

"Ouma," exclaimed Tania. "Mama was right, you're like a matchmaker from the Schtetl. Please excuse my grandma."

Mark took Ouma's hand in his, kissed it gallantly and winked at Tania.

Adam was already retreating. "Good to meet you all but you'll have to excuse me as I need to get to work."

Thembeki and Cook brought tea and cake, and Miriam introduced them. "We couldn't do without the help of these two wonderful women."

"Thembeki, please ask Michael to fetch the suitcases from the car and bring them inside."

"Yes, Miss Miriam."

"What was the journey like on the Union Castle liner?" Miriam wished she could trace every line on Joseph's face with her hand, and held back tears threatening to give her away. She tried to keep her hand from shaking as she poured the tea.

"Wonderful," he enthused, "until we hit the Cape of Storms. The sea was rough with huge waves."

"I was so scared the ship would sink and we'd all drown," Hannah joined in.

"In your last letter you said something about planting apple trees?" Joseph looked in the direction of the orchards.

Miriam moved her chair nearer to Joseph. "Yes, we've planted an apple orchard. We can take a walk there if you like after tea?"

"Good idea. We've been sitting in the car for too long. It'll be good to stretch our legs," replied Joseph.

Miriam felt his hand gently placed on her lower back as they started to walk. She held her breath and breathed out slowly.

They walked slowly, Joseph beside Miriam with Hannah, Mark and Tania following a step behind. Miriam broke the silence and pointed, "those are proteas, and we have a profusion of ericas and fynbos, all indigenous flowers."

Joseph knelt down to smell the fynbos, "Has a strong scent hasn't it?"

"Yes, snakes are fond of it too." Miriam laughed as Joseph got up quickly, and as he did so he picked up her wide brimmed hat that had blown off in the wind. Their hands touched as he gave it to her. She looked up at him and thought she saw something more in his eyes as he looked at her. They carried on walking side by side.

"Our apples have been picked and taken to the packing house. This is a busy time which is why Adam can't be with us right now. He'll join us later for a meal," said Miriam hoping he would be sober.

"What happens to the apples once picked?" asked Joseph.

Miriam felt herself tremble being so close to Joseph. "Apples are packed into boxes and taken to the railway station in Elgin, and then go by rail to Cape Town."

"I've seen Cape apples for sale in Covent Garden," said Joseph.

Miriam struggled to control the trembling. "Yes, we'll be exporting to England just like other farmers from this area. In fact the apples will be transported on one of the Union Castle Liners in refrigerated chambers. They're held in a cold store on the docks before being loaded on to the ship."

"How interesting," remarked Hannah lifting her white skirt so it didn't drag on the dusty ground, and catching up with Joseph linked arms with him.

They arrived at the orchard and Miriam pointed out the different varieties. "We've planted O'Heni Muri, Golden Delicious, Starking, White Winter Permain, Granny Smith and York Imperials."

"So many varieties? May I?" said Joseph as Miriam picked one off the tree and he took a bite. "Delicious," said Joseph offering the apple to Hannah who shook her head.

"That's a Winter Permain and my favourite," said Miriam. "We're trying the different cultivars to see which will be more disease resistant and do best. At least that's Adam's idea." She kept talking and chided herself for the feelings Joseph was arousing in her. She wasn't sixteen anymore. They reached the packing house where there was a tumult of activity. Women were grading the apples by hand and packing them in boxes. Box upon box stood ready to be transported by ox-wagon to Elgin station.

Mark smiled at Miriam before taking his mother by the hand, and walking down the line stopped to say a few words to one or two of the workers.

Alone for a few minutes Joseph took her hand in his. "Miriam, you know I've never forgotten our time together in the Schtetl."

She wanted to put her arms around him but instead asked. "Are you happy, Joseph?"

And sensed his hesitation.

"I have a good marriage. I'll always take care of Hannah."

Miriam felt his hand grip hers. "I still have the wooden heart you carved for me. I keep it on my bedside table."

He laughed. "My carpentry skills have improved a little since then."

But his laugh sounded brittle, and she felt a longing for what might have been. She took a step back and he released his hand. She dared not look at him for fear he might see what was in her heart.

"You'll never know ..." he began, but never finished the sentence as Hannah came striding up to them.

"I must sit down somewhere. This heat is oppressive," wiping sweat from her brow.

"I'm sorry Hannah, you must all be tired. We'll head back to the house and have something cold to drink. Cook makes a very good lemonade or maybe you'd like a glass of cold white wine?"

Joseph answered, "That sounds wonderful."

At the house they sat on the stoep whilst Joseph talked about his business. All the while Miriam sat opposite him lost in his every word, until Tania nudged her.

"Mama, Hannah is talking to you."

"Oh, sorry Hannah. I've just noticed Ouma falling asleep." Ouma's eyes had started to droop. "I think you need to have a rest Ouma." Miriam helped her out of the chair and to her room.

"When are they going?"

"Ouma, they've just arrived. They return to Cape Town tomorrow."

"Oh, thank goodness."

"Do you want supper in your room?"

"Ja, a good idea."

Miriam hurried back to the stoep. "Please excuse Ouma, she's not been well for some time. Tania why don't you take Mark for a walk around the farm?" Hannah was dozing off and Miriam felt relieved. Now she could talk to Joseph. "What is Mark doing now?"

"He's in charge of materials and designing our women's clothing lines. Since he joined me our shop has never done so well. As well as the factory, we have a shop in the main street of our village."

"But, I thought he was studying medicine?"

Joseph shook his head. "He decided he'd rather work in the family business."

They were silent for a moment. "I felt he made the wrong decision," said Joseph.

"It's hard being a parent Joseph. We have to let them make their own decisions even if we feel they're making a mistake," and wondered if Joseph was thinking about himself when he spoke.

Joseph pointed to Dominee who was inspecting his Ford motor. "Who is that?"

"Oh, that's Dominee. He's a Reverend at the local church, and he's part of the family." She couldn't help smiling at what was evidently delight on Dominee's face.

"A Reverend?" Joseph registered surprise.

"Hello there. Is this your motor car? What a splendid piece of machinery," Dominee shook Joseph's hand heartily. Hannah woke startled to find her hand in the grip of a Dominee. Miriam suppressed a laugh.

Miriam smiled at the merry party at her table that night. She sat at Joseph's side and they reminisced, interrupted only by Adam toasting their first shipment of apples. "They're probably going to England on the same ship as you," he remarked.

Tania looked askance at her husband always in a good humour when wine flowed freely.

"This is delicious. What do you call this dessert?" Hannah's voice rose in a crescendo after several glasses of red wine.

"It's Cook's baked apple tart. She's a wonderful cook and she could write a recipe book," said Tania.

Dominee was in high spirits, wanting to know about the family business in England. Without Ouma at the table, Dominee took it upon himself to serve the wine. Miriam felt flushed and intoxicated, and she knew it wasn't the wine. She couldn't believe a single day could go by so quickly. When the evening came to an end with the clock striking midnight, they bade each other goodnight. Joseph so near, yet he might as well have been thousands of miles away thought Miriam as she tossed and turned in bed. She heard the bathroom door open and shut. Footsteps stopped at her door and then silence. That night she dreamed Joseph was cradling her in his arms. All too soon the sound of the cockerel woke her. She made her way quietly to the kitchen needing a cup of coffee to clear her head after too many glasses of wine at supper. She heard footsteps and was surprised to see Joseph returning from an early morning walk. "Good heavens, you're up early."

"I didn't sleep well last night."

There was a moment of silence between them. Joseph stood looking at her with what Miriam thought were mournful eyes. Unspoken words like ghosts hovered in the air. To break the silence she blurted out, "Will you write to me Joseph?"

It was at that moment that Hannah joined them. "Where did you get to Joseph?"

He didn't answer Hannah. "Of course I'll write to you," and kissed her on the cheek.

Miriam felt herself tremble and dared not look at Hannah. She busied herself with the coffee, pouring a cup for Hannah and Joseph. She felt Joseph's eyes on her. She smiled at him wondering if she would ever see him again, and glanced at Hannah who was staring at them both.

She had managed to get through the night but had there been another night it would have driven her mad knowing he was so near. The situation was relieved when Mark and Tania entered the kitchen together.

"Why don't you visit us sometime Tania? I'd love to show you round," said Mark.

Miriam noticed how he looked at Tania who was blushing. Just as well Adam wasn't present. She was surprised at her daughter's enthusiastic response.

"Oh, I'd love that. Maybe when Daniel is older."

Tania's face mirrored her feelings. Miriam hoped hers didn't do the same.

Thembeki served breakfast and Miriam could feel Joseph looking at her. She tried to steady her hands but couldn't stop them from trembling. Nor could she stop the grandfather clock from chiming the hour of his departure.

After saying their goodbyes, Joseph hugged her until finally releasing her he got into the car. Miriam stood waving as tears poured down her face. Joseph hooted and revved the engine.

Tania put her arm around her mother. "He's a lovely man Mama. Here, take my handkerchief," and headed off to her pottery studio.

Miriam stood alone watching the car until it was no longer in sight.

OUMA ROSIE

Miriam met Dominee at the bottom of the stairs on his way up to see Ouma.

"Dominee, the doctor said Ouma's in heart failure, but she's still as stubborn as ever."

"I'll talk to her, don't worry, Miriam." He knocked on Ouma's door.

"Is that you, Miriam?"

"Can I come in, Ouma?"

"Oh, thank goodness, it's you. Come and sit down and maybe you can talk some sense into Miriam. She feeds everyone who comes to the door. Soon we'll have nothing left to eat." She pointed a finger at him. "It's your God who sent her to this farm."

"He's your God too, Ouma. You must trust Miriam. She hasn't failed you yet, has she?"

"Ja, ja, if you say so. Dominee, I must tell you about the angel who told me a long time ago in my dream that it was 'Time.' I didn't understand, but now I know she meant I'll soon lie side by side with my Jannie and Dirk."

"Don't talk like that Ouma. We all need you." He grasped her hand in his and wouldn't let go.

She carried on with laboured breathing. "Miriam has surprised me, making a success of running our farm. But don't tell her I said so, you hear. I'm worried how we're going to survive this depression."

"Ouma, you must rest. Let Miriam do the worrying."

"Ag, you know me. Dying doesn't stop me from worrying. I know the farm hasn't made much money this year."

"You have a young orchard, give it a chance. Besides, apples travel better than peaches. Farmers aren't having much success exporting peaches, seems they arrive in England dry and tasteless. You'll do better with exporting apples."

"We didn't plant peach trees. Maybe you need glasses. Look around, we planted apple trees."

His sigh was barely audible. "I hear there are problems with the cooling store at the harbour."

"So, what's being done about it?"

"Farmers demanded that the cooling store is investigated."

"Ag, you're so longwinded Dominee. I told you my time is up. I might not live long enough to hear the whole story."

He coughed. "Well, three scientists were appointed and they blamed rapid cooling at the harbour store."

She turned her head to one side closing her eyes. "I'll be dead before it's fixed. I must sleep now Dominee. All this talk makes me tired."

"Of course." He let go her hand and got up from his chair. "I'll come see you tomorrow, shall I?"

"As long as it's a short story."

That evening Daniel took a tray with supper up to Ouma placing it on her lap whilst Tania seated herself beside the bed, reading a book.

Ouma screwed up her eyes. "Shouldn't you be at school young man?"

"It's the holidays. Aren't you happy to see me?"

"Don't be cheeky young man," said Ouma. "What are you reading Tania?"

"I'm reading about Plaatje. An influential black man, Ouma. He spent his life in the struggle for the vote and liberation of his people."

Ouma coughed and spluttered all over the plate of food, but Tania continued. "Our country Ouma depends on us working together ..."

"Ag, why worry yourself about something you can't change?"

"Ouma, the black man was here before van Riebeeck set foot on this soil," said Daniel.

"Do they teach impertinence at your school?" She looked at Daniel above glasses that kept sliding half way down her nose. "I still remember some history even though I'm dying."

Tania saw Daniel's shocked expression. "Ouma's not dying, she just wants to shut us up. Why don't you go downstairs and let Ouma rest?" When he had left she turned on Ouma. "Why do you have to upset Daniel with talk about dying?"

"He sees birth and death all the time on the farm. What are you making such a fuss about?"

"I don't know why I come and sit with you."

"I told your mama she shouldn't have sent you to that English school. They put ideas into your head. Next you'll be telling me I should see a witch doctor."

"That's not funny, Ouma. If you treat the black man unjustly we'll all suffer."

"Why do you keep arguing with an old woman who's dying? You take after your mama not your pa."

Tania's voice had an edge to it. "I hope one day things will be different Ouma."

"Well, my child. I won't be around to see, as you put it. I haven't much time left in this world."

Tania closed her book with a thud. "We're outnumbered by the black man, in case you haven't noticed."

Ouma closed her eyes. "Next time, bring a different book with you."

Tania got up. "You can be so infuriating," and went out closing the door behind her.

♣ ♣ ♣

Ouma took to her bed from time to time, but this time she stayed in bed. Miriam called the doctor, worried Ouma was having trouble breathing.

Ouma opened her eyes when he arrived. "You're not a witch doctor are you?"

"Do I look like one?" he winked at Miriam.

"I can't see so well anymore, and I don't trust my granddaughter. For all I know she sees a witch doctor. How much "time" have I left doctor? I'm very tired." She beckoned to him to come nearer. "My angel seems to have got it wrong. She told me a long time ago my time was up."

Miriam was relieved to see the doctor smile.

"Well, that depends on you," he said taking out his stethoscope.

"I'm finished with work. I want to see my Jannie and Dirk."

His smiled faded as he listened to Ouma's breathing. Taking Miriam aside he spoke so that Ouma wouldn't hear. "Ouma has pneumonia. I'll check on her tomorrow and start her on sulphona-mide therapy."

Miriam turned away from Ouma, and held onto a chair to steady herself. "How serious is it, Doctor?

"Pneumonia is always serious. Keep her warm and see that she drinks enough. And, see that you get some sleep. You look ex-hausted."

Miriam sat by Ouma's bed for the next eleven days, with Domi-nee taking turns. She felt reluctant to leave Ouma's side but Dominee insisted. It was whilst Dominee was seated beside her bed and Miriam had quietly entered the room to take over, that Ouma opened her eyes. He leaned forward when she whispered. "No time now for a short story," her laugh was followed by convulsions of coughing. "Dominee, I'm going on the greatest journey of them all, aren't I?"

Miriam shivered and tried to block out the eerie sounds of the wind howling outside. It sounded as if the angel of death was coming to fetch Ouma.

"Dominee, I'm afraid. Will you stay with me?" He nodded gravely, held her hand and blessed her, taking a handkerchief out of his pocket to wipe his eyes.

Later that morning Miriam heard Ouma draw her last breath, and then all was quiet. She looked to Dominee who got up swiftly, took Miriam in his arms and together they wept.

The family walked slowly to the graveyard. Church bells chimed in the distance and filled the valley calling all those who knew Ouma Rosie. She was laid to rest with prayers by Dominee. He faltered now and again, and Miriam slipped her arm through his. Daniel held onto his grandma's hand whilst Tania and Adam stood beside her. Miriam couldn't imagine life on the farm without Ouma. She had grown to love her though she could be difficult and stubborn as an ox. It was Ouma who had been the driving force behind them planting an apple orchard. Now, she was the matriarch. They walked back to the farmhouse for the wake. Daniel didn't leave his grandma's side. "I'll look after you, Grandma."

Miriam hugged him. "You can look after me and this farm one day."

"That's double trouble Grandma."

For the first time that day Miriam smiled, and hugged her grandson.

Miriam tried to read between the lines of Joseph's letter that arrived shortly after Ouma's death. Just as she was sure his thoughts were of her, he mentioned Hannah, "his bride". His unfinished sentence when he came to visit, haunted her. What had he wanted to say? "if you only knew." In his letter he said he would always, "look after Hannah". Did he love Hannah? He wrote how he would remember their time in the Schtetl, even when he was an old man. But, it was his last words that never left her, "some things never die … just lie beneath the surface." She kept his letters together with the wooden heart in her drawer.

She was glad when it came to Daniel's school holidays. They went for long walks on the farm, and talked about what he might choose to do after High School. It took her mind off the past. Each morning when the first rays of sun shone through her window, she was up, breakfasted, before the family were awake. She waved to Daniel who had come out onto the stoep, as she made her way to the office.

♣ ♣ ♣

Michael came past the stoep, just as Daniel kicked a black spider tossing it high into the air. Daniel whipped round as Michael grabbed him by the arm.

"Hey, that spider isn't a rugby ball. You gonna kick everything that gets in your way?"

"It's only a tok tokkie," said Daniel shrugging.

"It starts with the small things." Michael released his grip.

"What are you talking about?" Daniel kicked a stone in Michael's direction.

"Respect for life, that's what I'm talking about."

"I get enough lectures from Ma and Pa, without you starting on me," scuffing his shoes as he kicked another stone. He walked off towards the barn where he waited for his friends. They sat in a circle smoking and lit a fire.

"You made out with Judith yet Danny?" Stuart sniggered.

"What's it to you?"

"Ha ha, I don't believe you have." Wynand slapped him on the back and laughed heartily. "Ag, Stuart man, leave the pisher alone."

Stuart threw his cigarette stompie over his shoulder. "Listen, if we don't talk about girls, how we gonna learn to be men?"

"Ja," answered Wynand. "You don't learn about sex in school do you?" his last words were drowned by a crackling sound.

Daniel turned round to see a bale of hay nearby had caught alight.

Michael hearing shouting coming from the barn looked in. "What the hell!" and barked orders. Together they lugged heavy buckets of water and doused the fire.

Daniel pleaded with Michael. "Please don't tell Pa."

"Well, don't ever smoke in a barn again, understand? And that goes for all of you. You boys better get off home now." Michael watched them scurry off like frightened rabbits. He walked Daniel back to the farmhouse in silence.

Daniel shivered as he said, "Thank you." He went indoors and passed Miriam as he went upstairs.

"Daniel, what's happened? You're wet and shivering."

"It's nothing."

"Must be something, because guilt is written all over your face. You can't hide anything from me. I know you too well." The story came tumbling out and Miriam listened without interrupting. "Thank goodness Michael was around. He's a good man Daniel. You can trust him. You've learned your lesson, so we won't talk about this again, and I won't say anything to your pa."

He kissed his grandma. "I promise I won't smoke in the barn ever again. I'll go change and join you for lunch."

Miriam made a mental note to speak to Michael, and suggest he take some time off to spend with Daniel. Adam was so involved in the farm he didn't have much time to spend with his son, and Tania was wrapped up in her pottery.

It was whilst Michael and Daniel were fishing one Saturday afternoon, that Cook happened to walk by. Daniel smiled watching Michael's eyes following the sway of Cook's well rounded buttocks.

"Hey, there's a big fish." Daniel pointed to Cook.

Next thing there was a pull on Michael's rod. He lost his balance, and fell into the river with an almighty splash. Holding his sides laughing Daniel helped him climb back onto the river bank.

"Man, why don't you just ask Cook out?"

Michael regained his composure. "I'm gonna reel her in slow like a big fish."

"Hope you're more successful than today," said Daniel grinning.

"Fishing is all about patience," said Michael.

"Ja, hope you reel Cook in before she gets away like the fish," and laughed at Michael's sheepish smile.

It was soon after that Adam took Daniel aside. "You're spending too much time with Michael. You need to inspire respect from our staff."

"You drink with him, don't you?" Daniel glared at his father.

That evening Adam brought the matter up with Tania. "It doesn't stop Daniel being friends with Michael for goodness' sake," she said in a huff.

"It's good advice I'm giving our son."

"You'd be better advising Mama to stop interfering in how we bring Daniel up."

"What has your mama ever done to make you think she's interfering. She adores her grandson. You're always so damn critical."

"For goodness' sake Adam, stop making that sucking noise with your teeth. Use a tooth pick. You do that to wind me up, don't you? Anyway, Daniel listens more to his grandma than to me."

"Then spend more time with him like his grandma does. I'm going to bed, I haven't time for this," throwing his newspaper on the floor.

"You're the right one to talk," and turned her back on him.

Miriam walked into the front room as Adam got up from the chair with a stern look on his face and strode past her. Daniel joined them, and Miriam could feel the tension in the air.

"Anyone for tea?" asked Miriam.

Daniel shook his head.

"Daniel, have you decided what you want to do now that you've finished High School?" Miriam glanced at Tania who was staring out of the window.

"I want to help you and Pa on the farm. I've decided to enrol in the Agricultural College. What do you think Ma?"

Tania turned round. "Fine by me, if that's what you want. I'm off to bed."

Miriam saw him flinch. "Your ma loves you Daniel, and your pa will be so happy that you want to work on the farm with him." She hugged her grandson.

There was a vacuum that was hard to fill for Miriam when Daniel was away at College. Cook and Thembeki continually hovered over her fussing. She ate Cook's dinners because she couldn't bear the long face when she pushed her plate away. One evening returning from the office, she stopped at the bottom step to the house wondering why she was so out of breath. There was that pain in her chest again. It was fleeting. Sitting at the table that night, her plate crashed to the floor as she slumped in the chair. Adam rushed to her side and Tania ran to phone the doctor.

Doctor Retief took one look at her and announced, "Bed rest for you, Miriam."

"What's wrong with me Doctor?" It irked her that Tania and Adam were whispering in the corner with the doctor. He hadn't appeared to have heard so she raised her voice, "What's wrong with me Doctor Retief?"

The doctor put his stethoscope away and sat himself down on the chair next to Miriam's bed. "You've had a minor heart attack, and it's a warning you need to take life a little easier."

"I've never been one to sit around and do nothing and I'm not about to start now." Miriam sat up straight in bed determined not to be treated like an invalid. She wasn't going to let a little chest pain get her down.

Doctor Retief looked at Tania and Adam, raising his eyebrows.

"I'll look in on you again Miriam."

"No need, I'll be fine and thank you for coming."

Tania saw him out. "You see what we're up against Doctor?"

He got in the car. "Perhaps you can help your mama in the office?" He didn't wait for a reply and drove off.

Miriam, after a few days bed rest, went down for breakfast and announced, "I must get back to work. Just hate the thought of work piling up on my desk."

Adam placed his hand on her shoulder. "You should listen to Doctor Retief and take things easy. I've been doing the books while you've been in bed. Everything's up to date. No need to worry."

"Thank you Adam but I'll take over now."

Tania cleared her throat. "Mama, why don't you listen for a change?"

Miriam ignored the comment, but couldn't ignore the feeling of unease always between her and her daughter. She turned to Adam. "I know you're quite competent to run the office Adam, but I'd like to keep my hand in. It gives me a reason to get up in the morning." Returning to the office, Miriam found she could only manage a half day. She made her way back slowly to the house and went to lie down. The next morning she spoke to Adam. "Can you take over in the afternoons?" She felt reluctant to let go the management of the farm when she'd worked so hard to build it up.

"Of course, Ma."

She kept telling herself she was still in control of everything. Walking slowly to the office she felt a little breathless. She gave little thought to her heart. The sun was up, the air was crisp and she was listening to her favourite music, the sound of bird song.

When Danny returned from college they celebrated his success at having passed his exams, and his pa took him aside to discuss the farm.

"What about Grandma. Why doesn't she join us?"

"Son, your grandma hasn't been too well lately."

"What's wrong with Grandma?" he said pouring his father and himself a glass of whiskey.

"She's had a minor heart attack." Adam put his head back and drank the whiskey in one go.

Daniel put his glass down. "Why wasn't I told?"

"We didn't want to worry you as you were writing your final exams. "Drink that down son."

Tania walked in and poked Adam in the ribs. "What did I tell you? You should have listened to me and told him."

"You both treat me like a child. Grandma must have wondered why I didn't come to see her." He stormed out and taking the stairs two at a time knocked on Miriam's bedroom door.

"Come in," Miriam called sitting up in bed holding a letter in her hand.

"Pa just told me about your heart attack. I didn't know Grandma. But now you can rest. I'm back and I'll help Pa run the farm."

Miriam held his hand. "Don't be angry with your pa. He only did what he thought was best. I'm so proud of you doing so well at college."

"Pa wants me to oversee the apple orchards, and he'll take over the financial side to ease your burden."

Miriam smiled. "It's never been a burden Daniel, but with the two of you running this farm I'm sure it'll continue to be a success. I've been just as stubborn as Ouma. It isn't easy to accept my old heart isn't doing its job properly."

"You'll never be old to me Grandma. Who's the letter from?"

"Oh, you're a nosey one aren't you? It's from Joseph."

"Who's he?"

"I grew up with Joseph in the Schtetl. He came on a visit a long time ago when you were a small boy. We've been corresponding over the years."

"For years! You're a quiet one Grandma. You never told me about him. Did you love him?"

"He was my first love and I've always loved him. One day when

I die, there's a little wooden heart he gave me that I want buried with me." Miriam pointed to the drawer where she kept it and Joseph's letters. Before Daniel had a chance to reply, she closed her eyes and was back in the Schtetl. She could see her home, the forests, and the lake where they had played as children. How many times had she re-lived that moment when Joseph kissed her and placed a wooden heart in her hand.

Daniel waited patiently. He placed his hand gently in hers taking in his grandma's face, now deeply lined and her once glossy brown hair was white.

She opened her eyes and spoke softly. "I remember overhearing my mama saying it was time to arrange my marriage. You see Daniel, marriages were arranged when I was a young girl."

"What happened?"

"There was a pogrom in the village next to us and we had to leave the Schtetl as soon as we could."

Daniel saw pain reflected on his grandma's face. "Would you have married Joseph?"

"There wasn't time. Our families had to leave the Schtetl in a hurry. We were sailing to South Africa. But, Joseph met a young girl, Hannah, on board the ship. She was on her own and promised him a job in her uncle's factory in England."

"What was she doing travelling alone? Didn't you need to be chaperoned in those days?"

"We didn't ask questions. My papa said that Joseph would have to support his family, and Joseph took the opportunity offered to him."

"Seems to me grandma, he let you slip through his fingers. Oh, by the way, there's someone special I want you to meet."

Miriam held his hands. "You've met someone. I want to hear all about her."

"Well, she's beautiful like you."

She laughed. "You know how to make an old lady happy. What's her name?"

"Judith Myers."

"A Jewish girl?" Miriam looked enquiringly at her grandson, and he nodded.

"Have you told your ma and pa yet?"

"Not yet. I wanted you to be the first to know."

"Is it serious Danny?"

"We've been going out for a few months."

"Well, I look forward to meeting Judith. Why don't you bring her to lunch on Sunday? All this talking is making me feel a little tired Daniel."

He rose quietly and Miriam closed her eyes. "I'll be back later to say goodnight Grandma." But she was already asleep and he tiptoed out of the bedroom.

THE SECOND WORLD WAR

Miriam propped herself up on the pillow, and beckoned Dominee to sit on the chair beside her bed.

"Dominee, you're an extraordinary man. You keep on going and look at me, another funny turn. I don't like seeing Doctor Retief kind though he is. He always prescribes bed rest. It's the one thing I dislike the most."

His face puckered. "My dear you ought to listen to the doctor. And, I'm an ordinary man. I don't have all the answers. Extraordinary is not how Ouma would have described me."

"Ouma welcomed you into this family, and that was extraordinary." They both laughed.

He sat up rigid when Miriam remarked.,"I'm not afraid to die Dominee."

Holding her hand in a tight grip. "You mustn't talk like that. You still have many years left to enjoy."

Daniel heard his grandma as he entered the bedroom. "Well Grandma, you'd better have Cook's soup before you exit this world, or she'll follow you into the next with a stick like she does poor Rusty."

Miriam laughed. "You see Dominee, no one takes me seriously."

"You're going nowhere Grandma. I'll see to that."

"None of us can play God young man." Dominee got up to go.

"No, you're right there. We're only human and can't stop the war that's heading our way."

"Whatever are you talking about?" Miriam wondered what on earth was the matter with Daniel today. He was always so optimistic about life. She saw Dominee's warning glance, and Daniel was looking grave as he sat down beside her.

"We heard Prime Minister Chamberlain on the radio. He's declared war on Germany."

Miriam shook her head not quite taking in what Daniel was saying.

Daniel's voice was hushed. "On the third of September, South Africa associated itself with the Allies."

"Oh, dear God not another war. Promise me you won't go fight Daniel." Miriam coughed to relieve the tightness in her chest.

Dominee lowered his head as Daniel answered. "I can't promise Grandma. I have to do my duty."

Miriam lay back when they had gone. She couldn't drink the soup Daniel had brought her. War had taken Dirk away from her. She couldn't face losing Daniel. The wind howled outside her window, just as it had done when Ouma was dying. "You're not going to take my Daniel." She shuddered and pulled the eiderdown over her head to drown out the sound.

Daniel volunteered for army service. When it came to say goodbye, Miriam held on tightly to his hand. He hugged her and whispered in her ear. "I'll write as often as I can," wiping her tears with his handkerchief. "Now you'd better let go of my hand because I'm going to need it."

Miriam couldn't manage a smile. "You see that you come back. Soon this farm will be yours."

Daniel squeezed her hand and moved on to kiss his ma. Tania

stood erect as a statue with her lips trembling unable to stop the tears when she hugged him.

"Come on son, we'd better get going. Your train won't wait for you." Adam threw a haversack onto the back seat of the car. They all gathered on the stoep to wave goodbye. Cook, Thembeki and Michael stood in the background. Daniel hugged Cook and Thembeki.

When he shook Michael's hand he felt something in his palm. It was a little wooden tok tokkie. "It's a lucky charm," said Michael.

"I'll keep it with me always." Daniel placed it in his pocket.

"Miss Miriam, it's cold. You should come inside." Thembeki covered Miriam's shoulders with a shawl. "Daniel's a strong boy Miss Miriam, he'll come back to us."

"He won't be a boy for long. The war will change that," said Miriam watching until the car was out of sight.

Thembeki helped Miriam to the lounge and on to a chair. Then went to the kitchen. "Cook, I want some soup for Miss Miriam."

"It's not supper time yet. What's the hurry?"

"Miss Miriam must have something warm to eat."

Cook shook her head. "It won't fill the emptiness she's feeling now."

Thembeki didn't have an answer.

Tania joined Miriam in the lounge. Miriam wanted to say something reassuring but Tania was hiding behind the newspaper. Miriam couldn't find the words to comfort her daughter. She leaned across and touched Tania on the arm. "We'll pray he returns safely to us."

Tania replied. "It'll take more than prayers for Daniel to return home safely."

Miriam struggled to eat the soup Thembeki brought her.

Tania put her arms around her. "Sorry Mama. I didn't mean to upset you, but I can't sleep at night worrying about Daniel."

"I know Tania. He's so young to be going to war."

Adam walked in and Tania turned on him. "You could have stopped Danny from volunteering. You could have talked him round."

"Calm down Tania. There's nothing I could have said to stop him. You should be proud of your son, isn't that so Ma?"

Tania broke down crying.

Adam put his arm around her. "Come, what you need is some wine to calm those nerves. You could fill the glass with all those tears."

Miriam closed her eyes finding it hard to see her daughter's distress, and wished she could have found words to comfort her. But, how could you reassure anyone in times of war. Like Tania she wished Daniel hadn't volunteered. She sat rocking back and forth, back and forth.

Adam put a glass of wine in her hands. "Here Ma, get this down you."

Thembeki fetched the soup dish and walked quickly out of the lounge to the kitchen. Cook for once said nothing when she saw the untouched soup.

♣ ♣ ♣

Daniel was sent to fight in Egypt in the tank corp. The family waited anxiously for letters.

"Thembeki, go tell Adam and Tania a letter has arrived from Daniel." Miriam sat down, her heart thumping in her chest. She didn't have to wait long for Adam and pointed to the letter. She waited nervously for him to read the contents. Tania arrived soon after out of breath. She stood reading the letter with Adam and her face lit up.

"He's been made a tank commander," said Adam proudly. "Wait, here are some photos of Daniel." They all poured over the photos.

"Daniel looks so handsome," remarked Thembeki, peering over Adam's shoulder. "But what is that Master Adam?"

"Those are boots sticking out of the ground," said Adam.

"We can see that thank you Adam. That's someone they've buried in a hurry Thembeki. They're fighting and there's no time to do things properly," said Tania.

"That's terrible Miss Tania."

"That's war Thembeki, and the death of hundreds of young men is the price we pay." Tania glared at Adam. "He's needed on the farm, before it turns into a desert like Egypt."

They were selling now to local markets, but like all local farmers were short of cash. The ships were commandeered for war. There was no space for fruit exports, and fruit threatened to flood the local market. Miriam waited for Adam each night worried their hard work would have been in vain.

Adam spoke of his fears. "The British Government have prohibited imports of deciduous fruit. All the progress we've made has come to a standstill because of the war. This could be a disaster for us."

Tania's voice was steady. "That may be, but the Deciduous Fruit Board has taken over, and we can sell our fruit to them, or the registered distributors. All is not lost."

"That'll be a wise move for us Tania." Miriam looked at her daughter in a new light. Perhaps Tania could be persuaded to take a more active role in the farm.

They lived sparsely, and were sustained by home grown vegetables and produce. A small herd of cattle produced fresh milk for the farm. The little they had they shared, and Tania made sure that their labourers didn't go hungry. Miriam watched the change in her daughter, especially Tania's excitement with the latest development by the Deciduous Fruit Board. One morning whilst having breakfast, Tania read from the newspaper. "Listen to this Mama. They're sending fruit all over the country in refrigerated railway trucks, and opening new markets for us on the East and West coast of Africa and the Middle East."

"Yes," replied Miriam. "It'll be a real boost for us fruit farmers," thinking all the time she hadn't heard them argue lately. Perhaps it had something to do with her handing over the running of the farm to Adam. It also made her happy to see a change in Tania's attitude. Adam needed Tania's support now that she was less involved. He was better at keeping the books and the practical side. Whereas Tania had a good overall perspective.

Miriam celebrated her 75th birthday with a quiet supper. When she unwrapped Tania's gift, she set it carefully on the table. "It's beautiful but what is it?"

"Can't you tell Mama? It's a sculpture of a nude woman in alabaster bending down and you only see her back."

She turned it round. "I love it Tania. I'll treasure it. Thank you."

Tania hugged her and Miriam felt close to tears. "I love sculpting Mama. It's something I'm good at."

"Tania, it's not the only thing you're good at. Look at the wonderful son you've brought up."

Thembeki and Cook joined the family to sing happy birthday. Returning to the kitchen Thembeki remarked. "Haai, Cook, did you see the present?"

"Hmph, if it was upside down I couldn't tell the difference. I don't know what goes on inside that head of Miss Tania."

They sat dunking rusks into tea until Thembeki broke the silence. "Miss Miriam hasn't had a letter from Mr Joseph for a long time."

"How would you know?"

"I take the post to Miss Miriam." Thembeki clucked and shook her head. "Ag, it's a shame about Miss Miriam and Mr Joseph."

"What are you talking about. He's married isn't he."

"Ja, but shame, I think Miss Miriam liked him a lot."

"You should've been a springbok. You're good at jumping to conclusions. Now you're wasting my time. I must get on and make soup. Find something useful to do instead of talking nonsense."

The war years took their toll on Miriam. She looked at herself in the mirror. Her hair was white, and her once proud posture gone.

Back problems caused her to walk with a stoop. She had to use a walking stick to maintain her balance. There were no more letters from Joseph and she put it down to the war. She was shocked one day when she received a letter from his son Mark to say his father had passed away. She sat holding the letter letting the tears roll down her face. Grief overwhelmed her. She couldn't bear to think she would never hear from him again. She'd cherished the few letters he'd written. To know she was in his thoughts was enough for her. There was an unbreakable bond between them though they led different lives. She thought of Papa, Mama and Ouma Rosie and how much she missed them. And now Joseph. It seemed almost too much to bear. A sense of loneliness overtook her and she wished Daniel was around to talk to.

Miriam felt a huge sense of relief when the war was finally over. She rejoiced when Daniel's letter arrived informing the family he was waiting for a sea passage home.

Miriam tried to quicken her step, hearing Adam's raised voice coming from the dining room. She leaned heavily on her walking stick as she stood at the door catching her breath.

"We need more labour. I'm employing black workers from the Transkei."

"What about their families? What about their women left alone in the Transkei?" Tania stared accusingly at her husband.

"It's only for the season Tania." Adam refrained from looking at her.

"It's the law Ma," said Daniel swallowing a piece of toast and coughing.

"Keep out of this Daniel." Tania's tone of voice could have cut through ice.

Miriam walked in having heard and sat down. "Daniel is right.

You might not like it Tania, but it's the law. Extra labour is needed, and it gives the men a way of earning money for their families."

Tania turned to Adam. "I hope you'll build a decent place for these black labourers to live."

"It's already under way," said Adam.

"Why didn't you tell me?"

"Tania, you're too busy doing other things these days." He grabbed his toast and headed towards the door.

"What exactly do you mean?" said Tania.

Miriam sat down watching her daughter's face turn a shade of bright red.

"You spend more time at sculpture or pottery classes, or whatever it is you do with that Matthew guy, than on the farm."

Tania sat glaring at him. "Matthew teaches sculpture and it's something I love to do. You know that Adam. Besides, I'm just as concerned as anyone else here about the farm."

Adam turned to Daniel. "I'll be fetching the men from the village of Mquanduli."

Daniel looked to Miriam. "What do you think Grandma?"

Miriam replied calmly. "You can't change these laws but we can treat staff fairly and decently."

"I notice you don't use the word equal Mama," said Tania.

Adam intervened. "Look, we don't make the rules and we have a farm to run. I haven't time to argue. I'm off to collect a new tractor. Want to come with me Daniel?"

"Sure thing." Daniel got up from the table with alacrity.

Miriam looked enquiringly at Adam. "You're getting a tractor?"

"We have to progress, and that means mechanization," he replied.

When they had gone, Miriam said, "We do what we can to help our labourers. You have a vote, use it," and sighed. She didn't have the energy to argue.

Tania flicked her hand upsetting a glass of orange juice. "I do, but then I'm white. The black man was given the vote by the British in 1854, abolished by our own people, General Hertzog in

1925." She turned on her heel, and walked out leaving Miriam staring after her.

Miriam heaved herself up from the chair and walked slowly out onto the stoep. Thembeki noticed Miriam sitting alone on the verandah with bowed head. "Miss Miriam, you look sad."

"Thinking of old times Thembeki." But she was thinking of Tania. She felt a sense of loss and failure as a mother. Being close to Daniel was a comfort and she treasured his company.

"I'll bring you a nice cup of tea Miss Miriam." Thembeki placed a shawl over Miriam's shoulders.

Next thing Miriam knew Cook placed a tray on the table with tea and rusks.

"You both fuss over me like two old hens," but she smiled at Cook appreciatively.

Miriam watched the progress on the farm from afar, still helping a little with the book-keeping. Adam always asked her to check his figures, even though she found them to be correct every time. More and more she left decision making to Adam and Daniel. After Adam's outburst she noticed Tania spent more time sculpting. Sitting on the stoep as she liked to do these days, she often saw her daughter with a basket of food, heading in the direction of the labourers' huts. Tania was stubborn and did exactly as she pleased just like Ouma.

Miriam remained silent when she came on the two of them once again in a heated argument, about the poor conditions Adam expected their black labourers to live in. It was Daniel who on this occasion entered the fray. "Ma, when we have enough money we'll improve their living conditions," and silenced his mother.

Miriam heard a new authority in Daniel's voice, and knew she had put all her apples in the right basket.

It was her 76th year and she was feeling more tired these days. She admitted to herself that the heart attack she'd had years ago had slowed her down.

Daniel persuaded his pa to buy him a second-hand motor bike with a side-car attached. "Come on Grandma. You have to see a beautiful sight. The spring blossoms in the orchards." He bundled Miriam into the sidecar and off they went.

Cook and Thembeki stood waving, whilst Tania with hands on her hips shook her head. "Ma is frail and Daniel takes her on an outing in that contraption?"

Adam laughed. "He wants her to enjoy herself. Nothing wrong with that, is there?"

"He should be taking young girls out and thinking of settling down."

"Oh, leave the boy alone. When he's ready he'll find a wife."

"That's just it, Adam. He's a man, though he doesn't behave like one sometimes."

Her eyes followed the contraption as it sent up dust in the air.

Miriam laughed at Daniel's exuberance. He roared down the orchard in between the apple trees with Miriam shouting. "Daniel, my hat." He stopped and lunged sideways grabbing it. They came to a halt where Daniel had placed a bench for his grandma. He helped her out of the sidecar and on to the bench.

"Daniel, I'm an old lady. You need a young girl to ride in this sidecar."

He whipped out a flask of tea and rusks, and they sat underneath the shade of a gnarled apple tree dipping them into tea.

"You don't need to tell me if you don't want to, but what happened to Judith?"

He looked down, silent for a moment. "Judith comes from a Jewish family. I don't think they accepted me when she told them Pa wasn't Jewish and you converted."

"Oh, but when they get to know you, they'll realise how lucky their daughter is. Besides, doesn't she have a mind of her own?"

"She won't go against her parents' wish."

"Do you love her?"

He nodded.

"Well then, that's all that matters. Talk to her Daniel. Don't let love slip through your fingers as happened to me. A lifetime of longing, can you bear that? Go to her now."

Daniel flew back to the farm with Miriam holding on to her hat and feeling each bump. She turned to get a last look at the pink blossoms adorning their apple trees. Depositing her on the stoep, he kissed her hastily, and flew off in the direction of Grabouw where Judith lived with her parents.

The family were sitting in the front room eating. Miriam smiled at her grandson.

"Glad you listened to me Daniel? What's it? Only a few months ago you flew like the wind to see Judith.

"Did you have to get involved Ma. Now poor Daniel has to convert to Judaism and be circumcised to please Judith's family."

"Oh, stop going on about it Ma. I'm being circumcised not you, and you haven't heard me complain," laughed Daniel.

"Oh, you will, you will," said Tania passing him a plate of eggs and bacon, and when you marry Judith, you'll have to forget about having bacon with eggs."

"Leave the boy alone," said Adam in a tired voice.

Thembeki who was serving in the dining room rushed into the kitchen throwing her hands into the air. "Oh Cook, have you heard? Our Daniel has to have a castration."

Cook frowned. "Whatever are you babbling about? Where did you hear such nonsense?"

"It's not nonsense. I heard Miss Tania say he had to be castrated before he gets married." She sat down hot and bothered, fanning herself with her apron.

"Oh, you silly woman. You mean circumcised, and it's only a snip and not the whole lot," said Cook, collapsing in a heap, and holding her large stomach laughing. "Haai Thembeki, life would be very dull without you. Where did your ma get you from?" She laughed till tears rolled down her eyes, and her stomach hurt.

"No need to laugh like that," said Thembeki stomping off in a huff.

Tania lay in bed waiting for Adam. "Adam, can we talk?" she whispered.

"What's the whispering for? No one can hear us."

Tania said nothing and waited for him to get into bed. She reached out to touch him. He turned away and switched off the light.

"Adam, why won't you talk to me?"

"I just have. Go to sleep."

"You know what I mean?" she touched him and he inched away.

"So, what am I now, a mind reader?"

"Why don't you want me to touch you?" Tania withdrew her hand.

"Oh, leave it alone will you."

"If you drank less maybe you'd be able to perform." She couldn't stop the words from tumbling out.

Adam was already snoring and she lay awake smelling alcohol on his breath. He was good at hiding his drinking. She turned away from him and curled up in a ball. The hurt at being rejected was worse than pain. It was months since he'd last made love to her.

Miriam leaned on her walking stick to catch her breath and peered into the kitchen. "Cook, we'll have fish for lunch when Judith's parents, Samuel and Rebecca, come on Sunday. I'd like you to make your wonderful apple pie and custard to go with it."

Cook beamed. "Certainly Miss Miriam."

When Sunday arrived, Cook was sweating with the exertion of frying all the fish. It was a hot day and she opened all the windows and the doors. She was shocked when Judith's mother walked into the kitchen unannounced, and spotted Cook as she looked around the kitchen. "I was looking for the lavatory. But, whilst I'm here perhaps I could ask if you keep milk and meat separately?"

Cook stood open-mouthed. Her eye caught sight of a fly and she swatted it with a vengeance. "You'd better ask Miss Miriam. The lavatory is at the end of the passage," and turned back to the stove.

Thembeki hurried into the kitchen to help, and found Cook muttering to herself. When Cook saw Thembeki, she exploded. "That blerrie woman. If she ever puts her foot into my kitchen again, I'll tell her to voetsak."

"What woman?" Thembeki stood a safe distance from Cook who was sweating profusely.

"Judith's mother," spluttered Cook. Saliva escaped from her mouth.

"What happened?" Thembeki asked moving well out of harm's way, and wiped spit off her face with the back of her hand.

"What happened?" Cook shrieked. "She asked, if I keep milk and meat separately? Why would I do that? Have you ever heard of such a thing?" Cook threw up her hands, and the fly swatter flew through the air.

Thembeki spoke as calmly as she could muster. "It's because they're kosher or something like that."

"I don't care what they are, but if she ever sets foot in my kitchen again I'll ..."

Cook stopped dead in mid-sentence with eyes bulging as she caught sight of Rusty. He had crept in quietly, and his head was just above the table inching towards her fried fish.

"Here, you evil dog. Voetsak before I separate you from that head of yours with my rolling pin." Rusty made a grab, and with a piece of fish hanging from his mouth tore out of the kitchen door with Cook running after him, waving a rolling pin in the air.

Miriam hearing a commotion, excused herself and made her way to the kitchen. "Thembeki, where's Cook?"

Thembeki pointed. "Chasing Rusty, Miss Miriam."

Miriam laughed. "He knows how good Cook's food is. Tell Cook I'll come and talk to her later." She walked slowly back to the dining room where the family sat having lunch. It was going well and they all seemed to get on, but she noticed that Tania was quieter than usual. Daniel dominated most of the conversation talking about the farm. The poor boy must be nervous. I must support him which his ma should be doing thought Miriam. "We've been talking about the farm all this time but what do you do for a living Samuel?"

"We have a hardware store in Grabouw. If you need any farming equipment we can order that for you. Get it at a better price too."

Miriam looked across the table at Rebecca,"Do you help in the business Rebecca?"

Rebecca's answer was swift. "Samuel has employees to help."

A brief silence ensued, and Adam passed the bottle of wine round. "Daniel why didn't you tell us we could buy from Samuel?" He spilt a little wine on the table as he topped up his glass.

"Daniel didn't know," said Samuel.

Miriam sitting next to Tania noticed Adam's hand shake ever so slightly, and Tania shift uncomfortably in her chair. She raised her glass. "Let's drink a toast to Daniel and Judith. To your engagement and future happiness."

After Judith's parents had left Miriam went to the kitchen, and heard the story from Thembeki. "Go tell Cook I want to talk to her."

When Cook came hurrying into the kitchen Miriam took in her stern look. "Sit down Cook. Thembeki told me what happened. I'm sorry, I should've talked to you sooner, but everything has happened so fast. Judith's family keep kosher, and they follow the dietary laws not mixing milk and meat. If Judith wants to keep kosher, we'll respect her wish. But, that doesn't mean all of us have to do the same, understand? I'm sure we can organise something. I'll ask Judith to come and talk to you."

"Thank you for coming to talk to me Miss Miriam. I didn't understand what … the woman … Miss Judith's mother was talking about."

"I wouldn't have expected you to Cook. Thank you for a delicious lunch. And now I think I'll go and have a rest."

After Miriam left, Cook poured a glass of leftover wine for herself and Thembeki and they did a jig in the kitchen.

"Just what I need after today. Daniel will need to be a saint to put up with his mother-in-law," said Cook. "Thembeki, sip the wine, don't swallow it like water. Savour the stuff woman."

"Ag, it feels so good. I'll have some more," said Thembeki holding out her glass and almost tripping over her feet.

When it came to Miriam's next birthday, the family gathered round for tea.

"Happy birthday, Miss Miriam," said Cook placing a birthday cake on the table.

"Oh Cook, what a beautiful cake. A chocolate cake, my favourite."

"Well, Grandma, don't just look at it, you've got to cut the first piece and make a wish."

"I wish the years wouldn't go by so quickly. Can I have another wish do you think?"

"You can have as many as you like Grandma."

"I wish to live long enough to welcome a great grandchild into this world."

Daniel smiled. "You'll have to be patient Grandma."

Cook had collected apples from the orchard that morning, and baked an apple tart. Thembeki's contribution was a tray of sandwiches from home-baked bread she'd made that morning.

Michael arrived to wish Miriam just as Tania handed her mama a present of another sculpture.

Miriam unwrapped the gift and set it down on the table to admire it. She examined the piece and then her eyes lit up "Oh, it's lovers in an embrace. It's beautiful. You are a gifted sculptor Tania."

"I express myself through my hands Ma and I love working with alabaster. It feels so sensuous," she said catching Adam's eye.

Cook nudged Michael and whispered in his ear. "Stop staring at the statue."

He glared at Cook, and when she and Thembeki went back to the kitchen he followed, "Don't you ever tell me what I can or can't do, do you hear?" he said. Cook took a step back. "You don't know your place. Who said you could go into the dining room?"

"I work for Master Adam, not you. So, where I go or what I do is my business." Turning his back on Cook he returned to the dining room where he and Adam discussed the day's tasks.

"Haai Cook, Tania is a better sculptor than farmer's wife."

"Watch your mouth Thembeki. Now come and help me."

"Help you with what? I've just finished doing the washing up and my legs won't hold me up anymore."

"Sit down and help me eat this chocolate cake and apple tart, silly woman."

They sat down with their feet up and helped themselves to large slices.

Thembeki with her mouth full of cake said, "I thought you and Michael ... you know?" and coughed as cake went down the wrong way.

"You thought wrong," said Cook and under her breath, "but I like a strong man." Cook ignored scratching at the kitchen door. "Suffer you evil dog," and tucked into another large slice of cake.

~ ~ ~

Shortly before the wedding, Miriam walked Judith around the homestead. While Judith stood admiring the wood furniture, Miriam paused to catch her breath. "It's a combination of mahogany and yellowwood. It gives the sitting room a feeling of warmth and cosiness, don't you think Judith?"

Judith nodded and walked over to the window. "The view of the mountain range is so beautiful from here."

"Yes, nature surpasses anything we can make, my dear. Come, I want to show you the bedroom we've prepared for you and Daniel. If you want to change anything you must say so." Miriam held on to Judith as they climbed the stairs.

Judith stopped at the door to the bedroom. "Isn't this your bedroom Miriam?"

"I don't need such a big room. Don't shake your head. I have a lovely room overlooking the orchards where I'll be very happy. Now, I want to know if you're happy with the changes we've made?"

A dolly varden dressing table was placed in front of the window bedecked in a bright yellow drape to match the curtains. A rocking chair stood in the corner. Miriam watched Judith's face as she looked around, and noticed her furtive look at the four poster bed.

Judith moved to the window. Orchards stretched as far as the eye could see, and beyond were the mountains etched in blue. "I wouldn't change anything. I love it."

Their reverie was interrupted when Miriam heard Daniel calling them for lunch.

Cook placed a dish of meatballs on the table. Miriam barely heard Judith whisper.

"Did you say something?" asked Tania.

Miriam sensed Judith tense under her daughter's gaze. "Did you want to say something my dear?"

"What meat did you use to make the meatballs?" Judith turned to Cook who was serving.

"Pork, Miss Judith."

"Oh … do you mind if I just have the vegetables? It's just that a dance teacher once called me an overstuffed meatball. Now I have an aversion to them."

Tania burst out laughing, and Miriam said, "What an awful thing to say. It would put me off eating meatballs too." She saw Daniel give his ma a withering look.

"Grandma, I must get to work. Please look after Judith." He kissed Judith. "I'll be back later to take you home," and hurried off.

Whilst Tania helped herself to tea Miriam took Judith aside. "Let's go sit on the stoep. Tania, are you going to join us?"

"In a moment Ma. I'll bring you and Judith tea."

Judith helped Miriam up and called out to Tania as they walked out of the dining room. "Thank you."

Once outside Miriam said. "I'm so sorry Judith. It's all my fault. I forgot to tell Cook you don't eat pork."

"I hope I haven't offended Cook?"

"I'll have a word with Cook, but you may want to talk to her yourself. Don't look so worried my dear. If you don't wish to eat pork we'll respect your wish."

"May I call you Miriam or would you prefer Grandma?"

"I think Miriam will do fine, don't you? I feel in my bones we're going to be good friends. Now tell me how your wedding arrangements are coming along."

They sat on the stoep and Miriam drew her shawl around her whilst Tania brought the tea placing it on the table.

"My parents want us to get married in the synagogue in Hermanus. Mother said we could have a tea afterwards at the Hermanus Hotel."

Tania frowned. "I offered to have the tea here."

Judith looked to Miriam, before answering in a faltering voice. "Mother thought it would mean less travelling for our guests."

"It's a long way for Ma to travel," said Tania.

"Tania, I think Judith's parents are very sensible. Don't worry about me. I would travel anywhere to see my grandson get married."

Tania stood up abruptly. "Such a pity. We could have a lovely wedding on the farm. Well, I must get on with my work. Would you like to come and see my latest sculpture Judith?"

Judith hesitated before she answered. "I'd like that."

Miriam called after Judith as she followed Tania, "When you get back, we'll go and talk to Cook."

Judith had a hard time keeping up with Tania, who was walking at a fast pace along a rough path alongside one of the apple orchards. They walked in silence until Tania finally called out. "There's the studio." The studio was a hut. Dust covered every conceivable space with the exception of the sculptures which were placed in a corner of the room. "Now you know where to find me, you're welcome any time to come and see my work."

Judith walked around and stopped to admire a piece of white alabaster. She ran her fingers over it feeling its texture. "What are you going to make with this?"

"Do you like the alabaster?" Tania looked up. She had already begun to work.

"It's beautiful," said Judith.

"Then I shall make something for you and Daniel."

"That would be lovely, thank you." Judith watched Tania's deft hands as she began work on the alabaster. "You're passionate about your work, aren't you?"

Tania replied without looking up. "It's my escape."

Judith folded her arms across her chest as silence settled in the room. "I think I should get back. Miriam is waiting for me."

Tania nodded and carried on working. Judith retraced her steps alone this time. She passed the labourers digging in fertilizer, and stumbled once or twice on the rough path. Looking up she saw Miriam sitting on the stoep waiting for her with Daniel. She hurried towards them a knot in her stomach, and wondered how she was going to get along living in the same house as her future mother-in-law.

"So, what did you think of Ma's work?" Daniel eyed Judith with a smile on his lips.

"She's going to make us something in alabaster."

"Is she now?" he replied.

"Judith, let's go talk to Cook. Daniel give me a hand will you?"

Daniel helped his grandma up from the chair and walked her to the kitchen. Cook was nowhere to be seen. Judith examined the kitchen more closely. There was a long table that stood in the middle of the room and she could smell freshly baked bread. The windows looked out onto a vegetable and herb garden. Cook's kitchen floors and surfaces gleamed.

"Cook is very proud of her kitchen," remarked Miriam. "I think we'll have to get help for Cook and Thembeki one of these days. They're not getting any younger. Perhaps you can keep it in mind Judith?" When Judith merely nodded, Miriam said. "You won't be stepping on Tania's toes, she's not the least bit interested in running the house. Do you help your mother in the kitchen?"

Judith smiled. "Yes, she's shown me how to make all the traditional dishes for the festivals."

"Good, then you can show Cook how to make them. It's a long time since I celebrated a festival."

"Will Cook allow me in her kitchen?" Judith asked.

"Oh my dear, Cook adores Daniel, and when she sees how happy you make him you'll walk right into that big heart of hers. Besides, it's your kitchen too whatever Cook might think." Miriam smiled at them both and Daniel squeezed Judith's hand.

It was the first time Miriam had been in a synagogue since they first arrived in Cape Town. She was transported back in time listening to the Cantor sing. She remembered as a young girl, searching for Joseph amongst the men sitting downstairs in the synagogue. When she spotted him she had given him a shy smile and could still see him wink back at her. She remembered her mama talking non-stop to Rachel. She thought about her silent prayer to God that she might marry Joseph one day. She asked her papa if God answered prayers. Her mama answered for him. She could still hear her mama's words ringing in her ears. "Don't expect an answer from heaven, it's up to you to make your dreams come true." Only she hadn't been able to, and had yearned for Joseph all her life.

She was roused from her thoughts when everyone rose as Judith entered the synagogue. She had never seen a bride look more beautiful. The wedding gown was adorned with lace and Judith wore a Juliet cap and veil. She remained seated as she couldn't stand for long anymore. The ceremony began with the recital of Psalm 100. "He who is mighty, blessed and great above all, may He bless the bride-groom and the bride." After more prayers, the bride and groom sipped wine and exchanged wedding rings. Miriam heard Thembeki gasp when Daniel stamped and broke the glass. The Rabbi reminded them this was because of the destruction of the Temple.

♣ ♣ ♣

"Haai, Cook. He could have got glass in his foot." Thembeki stood up peering over a large lady who wore an even larger hat.

Cook laughed at Thembeki's cross face. "Come, Master Daniel said we must look after Miss Miriam." They had brought a wheel-chair as Miriam could no longer walk very far.

The hotel decorated the reception room with proteas. Each table had flowers and surrounding the vases were small apples. Once the speeches were over Daniel and Judith took to the dance floor and then everyone joined in.

Cook laughed as she sat watching Daniel waltz Thembeki round the dance floor.

"I should sit down Master Daniel. These old legs can't move as fast as yours."

"Oh nonsense," but he took her back to her table. Thembeki flopped in to the chair out of breath, and looked up in amazement to see Judith and Daniel lifted in the air on chairs by the men. Judith gave a ribbon to several of her friends, and they danced round her plaiting the ribbons in a maypole dance.

Adam sat talking to Samuel and poured himself another glass of wine when Samuel took Tania onto the dance floor. Rebecca drew him into conversation about the farm as he topped up her glass. When Samuel and Tania joined them he poured more wine for them all. Tania sat down and hissed in his ear. "Why didn't you ask Rebecca to dance? And don't you think you've had enough to drink?"

Samuel and Rebecca were on the dance floor at that moment, and Adam ignored her comment. They sat in silence and Miriam having heard looked away, weary of the tension between them. She was grateful to Dominee who came to keep her company whilst watching the dancing.

"Ouma would've been amused to see you wear a yarmulka Dominee."

Dominee felt his head and took it off. "I put it on in the synagogue and forgot all about it."

Miriam listened to the music carefully and broke into a broad smile. Russian folk music was being played. Everyone returned to their tables when Russian tea and pastries were served.

Daniel bent over his grandma and hugged her. "I knew you would love this music Grandma."

Her eyes glistened as she held his hand in hers. "It takes me back to my youth Daniel. You should have seen Joseph do a Russian folk dance and I wasn't too bad either." She pictured herself and Joseph dancing together, so carefree and joyous. It seemed like yesterday, and Daniel's warm grasp felt just like Joseph's. She felt the familiar ache in her chest every time she thought of him. It never left her. It was there when she woke and when she went to bed. Only sleep had given her relief from the yearning. Was it to be like this till her dying day until she was brought back to the present?

Dominee raised his voice, "Miriam, did you hear what I said?"

She turned her attention to Dominee who chatted away, but part of her was still in the Schtetl with Joseph by her side.

Daniel had won over his in-laws. Rebecca hugged him. "I'm so proud you're my son-in-law. I always wanted a son you know."

"Well, now you have one Ma."

Miriam smiled at this exchange and looked over at Tania. It worried her how Judith would manage to get along with Tania. She was roused from her thoughts when Rebecca whispered in her ear. "I don't know where the caterer has got to?"

They couldn't help hear Tania's remark when she turned to Adam. "I told you we should have had the wedding on the farm."

Rebecca turned back to Miriam. "Do you think Cook could help? Not everyone has had tea and pastries."

Miriam heaved herself up. "Come, we'll go have a word with Cook."

"Miriam, don't you need the wheelchair?"

Miriam shook her head. "I can manage to walk as long as it's not too far."

Cook stood surveying the chaos in the kitchen. She started going through boxes, throwing away empty ones and finding those containing the pastries.

She hurried over to Thembeki and pulled Michael up by his jacket sleeve, "Come help." It was an order. Later that afternoon Cook allowed the staff to sit and enjoy tea with the left over pastries.

"It's not too bad working with you Cook. It has its rewards, tea and pastries." Michael winked at Thembeki, but his smile was wiped off his face by Cook's black look. He walked out shrugging his shoulders, "Can't please you."

It had been a long day for Miriam. It was clear to see that Samuel and Rebecca adored Daniel and she watched her grandson with pride. He came with Judith to say goodbye as she was ushered into the car.

Rebecca came rushing over. "Cook, please accept this," and placed an envelope in her hand. "It's for all three of you. Thank you for helping out."

Cook looked at the wad of notes. "Thank you, Miss Rebecca."

Miriam returned home with Cook, Thembeki and Michael who was driving. Cook divided the money and then looked at Michael. "You sure you haven't had too much to drink?" He didn't answer. "Like that caterer I saw sitting outside half drunk."

"Thank you for saving the day Cook, and you Thembeki, and Michael." Miriam closed her eyes going back to the past. It was starting to get dark and they had a long way to go. She dreamed Joseph came to fetch her and felt his hand in hers. Waking up she stared out of the window whispering. "One day, it'll be our time."

Sometime after the wedding the family were at lunch. Miriam noticed Adam looking surly, and there was silence at the table. She glanced at Judith and could almost feel her discomfort, whereas Daniel seemed unaware of any tension, and was attacking his food. The atmosphere was so uncomfortable she said the first thing that came to mind. "I see you're selling to hawkers. How are they paying you Adam?"

He answered abruptly. "It's substandard fruit that we can't export, and they pay cash."

"It was my idea Grandma." Daniel looked up at his pa's tone of voice.

"I see." Miriam wondered what was troubling Adam.

Another silence and Miriam noticed Judith pushing food around her plate. She saw Daniel reach for Judith's hand. Just then Cook entered with dessert of stewed apples and custard.

Miriam beckoned to Cook who helped her up from the chair. "I'm feeling rather tired. I think I'll go and have a rest."

"I'll help you to your room Grandma."

"I think I'd like Judith to help me, if you don't mind Daniel."

They walked slowly along the passage whilst she leaned on Judith for support. Once in bed she held Judith's hand. "You'll get used to this family. I remember when I first came to live here as a newly wed. I was scared of Ouma Rosie, and she became like a second Mama to me. Not that it was always easy living with such a stubborn old lady."

Judith put the eiderdown over Miriam. "You mustn't worry about me. I'll be fine."

Judith tip-toed out of the room leaving Miriam asleep and headed for the kitchen. She peered in at the doorway. It was Cook who saw her first. "Would you like me to bring the tea, Miss Judith?"

"Do you mind if I have tea here?" She sat down inhaling the smell of baking bread.

Cook and Thembeki exchanged looks. "Of course, Miss Judith. Would you like a piece of cake with your tea?" Cook moved into action.

Judith's words were almost a whisper, "Yes, thank you."

"Miss Judith, you'll get used to living on a farm," said Cook placing a cup of tea on the table.

Judith took a deep breath. "I'm sure I'll get used to it Cook. Everyone calls you Cook but do you have another name?"

Cook's eyes turned to slits as she gave Thembeki a warning look. "My real name Miss Judith is Chipo. It means 'gift' but friends teased me and shortened it to Chips, so I stuck to Cook."

"I think it's lovely and you're a gift to this family Cook," she paused whilst Thembeki had a coughing fit. "Are you alright Thembeki?"

Thembeki swallowed some water and nodded.

"Cook, I need your help to make some traditional dishes. Could you spare some time?"

Cook replied briskly.,"Of course, Miss Judith."

"Could we make a start tomorrow, as the Jewish New Year is soon."

"Certainly Miss Judith," replied Cook smiling broadly.

Thembeki looked puzzled. "But New Year is the first of January Miss Judith."

"It's the Jewish New Year Thembeki, when we pray for forgiveness, and to be written in the Book of Life for the following year."

Thembeki answered in a serious tone of voice. "Will you pray for Miss Miriam?"

Judith looked at her downcast face. "Of course, Thembeki. Thank you for tea Cook. I'd better go now. I'm not feeling so good."

♣ ♣ ♣

Thembeki's face lit up. When Judith left she turned excitedly to Cook. "Do you think she's pregnant?"

"Hold your tongue woman."

"I can tell you know," said Thembeki.

"Oh, so now you're a fortune teller?"

"You'll see. Just remember my words," and began to sing as she washed up. Cook winced attending to the washing. She took the wet clothes and went to hang them out cursing Rusty as he got under foot. "Voetsak, you miserable thief." Blinking, as a raindrop fell on her nose. Cursing for Africa, she started taking in the washing she had just finished hanging up.

Michael passed laughing. "Weather got the better of you Cook?" and carried on walking turning to smile showing teeth that were missing.

Cook threw him an angry look, threw the washing in her basket, and hurried indoors.

In the following months Miriam began to feel more short of breath. Thoughts went round and round in her head. Tania as usual spent most of her time at sculpture classes or in her studio away from the farm. She decided she must speak to Judith one brisk September morning, and asked to be taken for a walk to see the spring blossoms in the orchards. Judith wrapped a blanket over her.

"Judith take me to Daniel's bench."

Judith pushed the wheelchair along the path between the rows of apple trees.

"Did Daniel ever tell you that it was whilst we sat on this bench that I encouraged him to go to you?"

Judith sat down, putting the brake on the wheelchair. "You're behind everything that happens on this farm."

"Well, that's what I want to talk to you about."

"I wondered why you wanted to come all this way?" helping Miriam out of the wheelchair and on to the bench.

"This is my favourite spot, especially in spring. It's peaceful and a good place to talk away from everyone." Miriam sat looking at the trees now in full bloom and giving off their sweet earthly scent. "Daniel chose well."

"He certainly did. This is a beautiful spot," said Judith.

"No, Judith. I meant you. When I die one day …" Miriam began. Judith put her hand up. "Please Miriam, don't talk like that."

"I'm getting old, my dear."

There was an eerie silence. Judith reached for Miriam's hand.

"I'm not afraid of dying Judith. There's something out there in the universe beyond our understanding. My dear Judith, you'll have to forgive me for rambling on, but something tells me you'll understand." Miriam felt almost as if the Hand of God was shading them, except when she looked up there were dark clouds gathering overhead. "Now, let me talk about more practical matters, this family needs a woman who can take over from me and run the home."

"Are you asking me to do so?"

"Yes. It would make me very happy."

"But what about my mother-in-law?"

"My daughter isn't interested in running a household. I think I mentioned it before. You must have realised that by now. "

Judith hesitated for a moment. "I wouldn't want to offend her."

"Don't worry, she'll be happy not to have the responsibility." Miriam looked up as she felt a drop of rain. "How fast can you push me?" they both laughed as Judith helped her into the wheelchair and back up the path. Miriam pointed out the spring flowers along the way. "Thanks to the rain our fields are covered with flowers, just look Judith." Daisies had sprung up everywhere spreading themselves like a blanket over the earth as far as the eye could see. As they neared the house Miriam suddenly thought of Dominee. "Judith, there's one other thing I must mention and that's Dominee. You know he's been a part of this family since Ouma's days. He's an old man now but promise me you'll include him in everything."

"Of course, you don't need to ask."

Miriam looked with pleasure at their Cape Dutch homestead

with its gables and green shutters. "My dear, I hope you'll be as happy as I have been on this farm."

~ ~ ~

A dream of a seed / Bearing golden apples / Grew upon fertile ground.

Tania supervised the school for the labourers' children, and asked Judith along one day. The women walked past the lake and orchards at a brisk pace with the sun high in the sky.

"You never talk about what you do on the farm," said Judith peering into the classroom where there were two children to a desk with one textbook between them. Their teacher was busy writing on the blackboard, and turned to wave to Tania.

"Let's not disturb them. I don't talk about what I do because I don't think anyone is interested. Take Adam for instance. I struggle to get money out of him to improve facilities for our labourers."

"I think you're doing a wonderful job."

Tania's face lit up. "Would you like to help me?"

"I'd like that very much."

"Good. What we need is more money to pay our teacher, Mr Dalitso. He's threatened to leave his post for a better paid job. I'm desperate to hold onto him. He's been such a good teacher and a blessing. Funnily enough that's the meaning of his name."

"I'll have a word with Daniel," said Judith.

Tania thumped her on the back. "Now, why didn't I think of that? You clever girl."

They carried on walking and Tania pointed to the labourers' cottages. "What they need are toilets inside their houses."

"Where are the toilets?"

"Behind the houses, and they're shared by several families. Cheaper that way, according to Adam. So, you can see changes are needed."

Judith nodded in agreement and looked at sheets billowing in the wind with hens darting in between them. A few women were sitting on doorsteps chatting and waved to them as they passed. They passed rows of cottages surrounded by bare ground and dust, and they made their way to the orchards where they stopped for a while. Tania spread a rug on the grass, and brought out a flask of tea with some of Cook's homemade biscuits. Judith wolfed them down in a matter of minutes. It was pleasant in the late afternoon and they watched the sun paint the sky a glorious orange as it dipped below the horizon.

"Tell me Judith, how are you finding life on our farm? It must be so different to what you've been used to?"

Judith hesitated before answering. "It's been easier than I expected, and I don't care where I live as long as I'm with Daniel."

Tania pursed her lips. "I remember once feeling the same. Anyway, I think we'd better get back and see how Ma is doing. She's so frail these days."

Judith hoisted herself up. "I'd better see how Cook is getting on. I asked for her help to prepare for Rosh Hashonah."

Tania rolled up the rug. "Ah yes, the Jewish New Year."

Judith's voice was hushed. "I didn't think you'd mind? I mean, celebrating Rosh Hashonah."

Tania put her head back and laughed. "Why would I mind? We'll get to taste traditional dishes. It'll be a welcome change from Cook's menu as good as she is."

Cook was in the kitchen with steam rising from a pot on the stove and perspiration dripping off her.

"Miss Judith told me that on New Year all mankind is judged for its fate in the coming year. That means I'm also going to be judged by God, and God counts your sins," said Cook wiping sweat off her brow with the edge of her apron.

Thembeki stood hands on hips smiling. "You turned Jewish Cook?"

Cook was about to open her mouth but just then Judith opened the kitchen door slightly out of breath.

"Sorry to be a bit late Cook," and went straight to the stove to check the cooking. "That's wonderful Cook, you don't even need me," she said but slipped on an apron. Together they made chicken soup; chopped liver and perogen. Cook made an extra large apple tart to end the meal.

"Cook, I'm going to lay the table." Judith hung her apron on the hook behind the kitchen door.

Thembeki shrugged and was just about to pop a meat pie in her mouth when Cook slapped her on the wrist. "Those perogen are for the soup," moving the dish out of reach.

"You don't put meat pies or whatever you call them into soup," exclaimed Thembeki and proceeded to pop another one into her mouth. "Miss Judith won't have counted them," licking her fingers. She moved swiftly and was out of the kitchen faster than Rusty could run. She found Judith in the dining room. "Oh, Miss Judith, the table looks beautiful with flowers and all the silver."

Judith placed two candles in the centre of the table. "Something's missing Thembeki. Ah, it's honey for dipping the apples in. Would you get some from the kitchen please."

Just as Thembeki was about to enter the kitchen, she overheard Cook talking to a man. His voice sounded familiar and she stood quite still out of sight.

"What do you want? I'm very busy now." Cook's voice was a pitch higher than usual.

"Be nice to me Cook. I've come to ask you to the dance."

Thembeki put her hand over her mouth to stifle a laugh.

"There's plenty women out there, so don't come into my kitchen and waste my time."

"Yes, but how many of them cook as well as you do.?"

Thembeki heard Cook shout. "Take your feet off my chair. Don't you have a job to do? I'm busy now."

She heard the back door slam shut and sauntered in smiling.

"What are you smiling about?" barked Cook.

"Was that Michael?"

"What's it got to do with you?"

Thembeki played safe. "I've come to get some apples and honey for the table." She looked at Cook's flushed face and impulsively asked. "So, are you going to the dance with him?" One look at Cook's thunderous face made her grab the apples and honey and make a quick exit. She didn't look back as the kitchen door slammed behind her.

Miriam sat up in bed as Thembeki placed a tray of tea on her bedside table. She was not feeling well but insisted she didn't need a doctor.

"Thembeki, I've heard there's going to be a dance in the barn. Are you and Cook going?"

"No one has asked me Miss Miriam."

"Oh, what a shame. What about Cook?"

Thembeki smiled. "I think Michael's invited Cook but you mustn't tell her I told you."

"I won't breathe a word. But, I thought Cook didn't get on with him?"

Thembeki shrugged her shoulders. Miriam looked at her downcast face. "You never know, you might meet someone. Why don't you go?"

"I'm too old Miss Miriam."

"Nonsense. You're never too old for love. Thank you for the tea Thembeki. I think I'll have a rest now before dinner," leaning back on her pillow she closed her eyes.

That evening the family enjoyed a traditional Jewish New Year dinner. Miriam sat on her grandson's right in her wheelchair. It felt frustrating not being able to walk a few steps without becoming short of breath. But, she was adamant she was not going to miss this auspicious occasion, and was happy that Judith remembered to ask Dominee.

Daniel stood up to make a toast. "I hope we celebrate many more special dinners in the years to come." He raised his glass. "To Grandma, long may you boss us around."

Miriam laughed but her eyes filled with tears when Daniel kissed her.

Then he added. "A special thanks to Cook and Thembeki and Judith for the wonderful food we've enjoyed tonight." He grinned at Cook who had caught him giving a little piece of his perogan to Rusty.

"Hear, hear," responded Dominee raising his glass.

Miriam excused herself after dessert, and as Thembeki was pushing the wheelchair out of the dining room, Dominee called after her. "I'll come up if I may and say goodnight in a short while."

Dominee sat on the chair next to Miriam's bed. "You must be proud of Judith and Daniel. He conducted the service just as I expect a Rabbi would and the food," he paused ... "was very tasty."

Miriam replied in between breaths. "I've long forgotten ... how my papa ... conducted a Rosh Hashonah supper ... but Danny did a fine job tonight."

Then she clasped his hand. "Promise me Dominee you'll always be there for Danny when I'm gone."

Dominee nodded and his grip tightened on her hand listening to her breathing.

"Don't look so sad Dominee, my life has been a long journey, and I'm ready to go on the next." She felt a comforting silence between them.

A few days later, Thembeki knocked on Miriam's door. There was no answer. She opened the door quietly. Then she heard a cough.

"Oh, I'm so glad to see you Thembeki. Put the tray on the table and sit down."

"Miss Tania said I mustn't tire you by talking too much."

"Oh, don't listen to her, such nonsense." Miriam broke into a coughing fit frightening Thembeki who ran to find Tania and bumped into Judith on the way.

"Miss Miriam can't breathe," said Thembeki and burst out crying.

Judith hurried to the bedroom and made Miriam take a sip of water. "I think we should call the doctor." She felt Miriam's forehead which was clammy. She managed to get Miriam to take another sip of water and made her more comfortable.

Dr Retief came later that day. After examining Miriam he took Judith aside. "See that your mother-in-law rests Judith. I'm afraid her heart is failing." He closed his medicine bag. "I'll look in on her tomorrow. I'm off on my rounds but before I go I want to ask that nice Cook of yours if she has any leftover apple tart for me."

Judith took him to the kitchen where he greeted Cook and asked politely, "Can I have a slice of your wonderful apple tart Cook?" Before she could reply he opened the fridge, and helped himself. Cook stood respectfully aside.

"Wonderful Cook," he said with a mouth full. "Wish you could teach my wife how to bake," helping himself to another slice he took his leave.

Thembeki stood wide-eyed at the back door watching Michael march up the path. Judith retreated closing the kitchen door quietly as Michael sauntered in to the kitchen. He sat down and Cook gave him tea and a slice of her apple tart. Thembeki grabbed the washing, and hurried out of the kitchen tripping over her feet as she looked back at them.

Judith returned upstairs to Miriam to find her sleeping. She wondered where Tania was and went to ask Thembeki to call her. Walking into the kitchen she came across Cook and Michael deep in conversation.

"Do you know where Thembeki is Cook?"

"Gone to hang up the washing Miss Judith."

Thembeki was in the back yard, and Judith was about to call out when she suddenly felt dizzy. Thembeki came running and caught her before she hit the ground.

"Miss Judith, should I get Master Daniel?"

"No, no. I'll be alright in a minute. Will you give Miriam her medicine when she wakes up? And do you know where Tania is?"

Thembeki shook her head.

"Don't look so worried Thembeki. I'm alright now, but I must find Daniel to tell him about his grandma. I'll just sit down for a few minutes and catch my breath."

Thembeki finished hanging up the sheets, peering around to check on Judith. By the time she was done Judith had gone. Thembeki bypassed the kitchen and went in the front entrance. Going up the staircase she caught sight of herself in the hall mirror and muttered under her breath. "I'm slimmer than Cook with her tree trunks for legs." She hitched up her skirt to inspect them in the mirror.

"What are you doing?" grinned Daniel.

"Oh, Master Daniel, Miss Judith said I must give Miss Miriam her medicine."

"Go make us some tea and bring it upstairs. I'll see to my grandma," and watched Thembeki scurry off with her face all flushed.

Thembeki stood outside the kitchen door, and not hearing anything opened it to find Cook and Michael in an embrace. She coughed, unable to move.

"What is it?" Cook asked in an exasperated tone.

"Master Daniel asked me to make tea."

"Well, get on with it," said Michael, slapping Cook on the buttocks and winking at her as he left by the back door.

Thembeki made the tea and the only sound that could be heard was Rusty scratching to be let in. She kept taking furtive looks at Cook. How did Cook who was getting on manage to get a younger man? She couldn't quite believe it especially as Cook had treated him real mean.

Daniel sat down quietly by Miriam's bedside with bowed head. He felt a hand touch his.

"Danny," Miriam said breathing heavily.

"Yes Grandma?" his eyes smarting with tears.

"I've seen Joseph ..." she paused to catch her breath and whispered, "Joseph is waiting for me ... I remember the Rabbi once saying there is no death at my papa's funeral. You see Daniel, we're not alone when we die."

"Don't talk Grandma, you're exhausting yourself."

"Danny, can't you see Joseph?" Miriam half raised her hand to point but the exertion was too much.

Daniel squeezed her hand and hugged his grandma. "You're as light as a feather Grandma," and kissed her cheek.

Each morning he went to sit with Miriam. She spoke less and less as her breathing deteriorated. When he got tired, Judith and Tania took it in turns to sit with her.

One morning Judith whispered. "I'm pregnant Miriam," and wiped away tears as Miriam seemed not to have heard. She bent over Miriam to kiss her.

Miriam heard only the howling of the wind but this time she wasn't afraid. She felt a sense of joy for she could see Joseph waiting with outstretched hands. She lifted her hand towards him and whispered, "Joseph."

BIBLIOGRAPHY

"Apples of the Sun" by Phillida Brooke Simons. Fernwood Press Haeberg.

"The Story of the Apple" by Barrie E. Juniper & David J. Mabberley. 2006, Timber Press Inc.

"Shtetl" by Eva Hoffman. 1999, Vintage.

"The History of the Jews in South Africa" by Louis Herman. South African Board of Deputees.

"Western Civilization and the Natives of South Africa" edited by I. Schapera. 1967, Routledge & Kegan Paul Ltd.

"Legislation & Race Relations" by M. Horrell. 1971, South African Institute of Race Relations, Revised Edition.

"The Jewish Religion" by Louis Jacobs. 1995, Oxford University Press Inc. New York.

"The Virtual Jewish History our South Africa" by Rebecca Weiner.

"Oudtshoorn The Jerusalem of South Africa" in *The Jerusalem Post* by David Zetler, 25 Jan 2007.

"South Africa – History" – 1996-2006

"Cape Town" by Jean Morris (text Jessica Abrahams). 1979, Don Nelson Cape Town.

"Pictorial History of South Africa" by Antony Preston. 1989, Central News Agency Ltd, Bison Books Ltd.

"Tip and Run" by Edward Paice. 2007, Weidenfeld & Nicolson.

"The War Reporter" – The Anglo-Boer War through the Eyes of the Burghers J.E. Grobler. 2004, Jonathan Ball Publishers (Pty) Ltd.

"Black Monday Lovesong" by A.S.J. Tessimond in *Poetry Please*, 2002, The Orion Publishing Group.

Websites:

http://www.southafrica.com/northerncape/kimberley/magersfontein

http://www.answers.com/topic/battle-of-magersfontein

http://www-answers.com/topic/second-boer-war – Second Boer War

http://www.spartacus.schoolnet.co.uk/Whobhouse.htm – Emily Hobhouse 'The National Archives Learning Curve'